GORILLA IN THE HISS

A FUC ACADEMY STORY

JODI KENDRICK

ACKNOWLEDGMENTS

THANK YOU!

To my family, friends and writing community.

Your continued love, support and encouragement keep me going. Without you, I'd still be dabbling and drifting.

John & Kevin – for the extra eyes on the rough spots.

Kim – for cleaning up my messy language.

Jess – for the doors you've opened for me.

To **Eve Langlais** – my deep appreciation for your generosity in opening your creative world.

For Emily.

TERRY
FAMILY

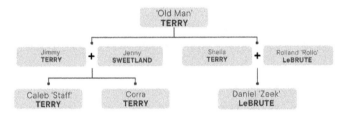

Katz stifled a yawn as she rushed along the path from the Furry United Coalition Newbie Academy—FUCN'A—housing to the Working and Administration Networking Core—WANC—building.

Day one of the new job.

Swiping her clammy palms across her thighs, she smiled at the cluster of students she passed on the steps up to the door.

First day and already late.

It couldn't be helped. She'd had to delay her flight.

Mummy had needed her for a last-minute meeting that ran late into the night before she was due for another round of negotiations on *another* business deal on the other side of the world.

Exhausted and impatient, Katz had initiated a lengthy *disagreement.*

Katherine Karak knew her mother was actually attempting to sabotage Katz' choice to work for the FUC Academy for a couple of semesters. The late night had ended in a volatile argument. It was uncharacteristic for Katz to engage in full-on confrontation with her predatory mother.

But that was last night.

She'd caught a red-eye and arrived but had managed only a few hours' sleep.

"So I was inspired by my brother Darcy's ability to break free of our parents' plans to bind him to the family business." In her nervousness, she'd been explaining this to the administrative secretary, who stared expressionlessly at Katz.

Her lioness mother was a CEO and owner of a corporation that specialized in mergers, acquisitions and management consulting. She had her claws in every aspect of the family business—including her children's private lives.

"Lovely," the secretary said in a pinched voice. "Please complete these forms while I retrieve your employment package." She rose from behind the desk, gaze flicking up and down Katz. "This was due last week. Further tardiness will not be tolerated, Ms. Karak."

Typical WANC'er.

Snatching a pen from the countertop, Katz moved toward the windows with their wide ledges that stretched toward the ceiling, resting the clipboard and forms against one ledge for better visibility and to catch a bit of sunbeam-basking while she worked.

She drew a deep breath and began filling in the forms.

Katherine Karak. Twenty-three. Shifter type—Feline. Was that enough, or did they need specifics? Caracal. Next of kin... Darcy Karak, brother, shiny new FUC agent.

"That will piss Mother off—to not be named as my next of kin," she muttered, tapping her pen against the clipboard.

Former employment. Family business—lifetime.

She drew a deep breath to dispel the encroaching sense of suffocation that the idea of spending her life working in the family business, without any modicum of autonomy, brought.

"All this is in my resume. Why do I have to fill this out again?" she grumbled then glanced back toward the counter to ensure the WANC lady hadn't heard her, not wanting to erode her first impression further.

She put the pen on the ledge and pinched the bridge of her nose.

Katherine, you know you're no good without a solid ten hours of sleep. You'll never make it through the day without chomping someone.

She glanced at her watch.

How long till nap time?

Hours still.

Eyes closed, she turned her face upward, soaking up the morning rays streaming through the glass.

"Nearly finished?" The WANCer's clipped voice startled Katz, interrupting her purring.

Her eyes snapped open and turned down to the forms. No. "Yes, ma'am."

She raced through the rest of the questions, belligerent muttering sprinkling her space under the window.

She turned on her heel, plastering her professional smile across her face as she approached the desk to deposit her completed forms.

The woman slid a fat envelope onto the counter, and Katz' clipboard disappeared behind the barrier. "Everything you need is in there. Your schedule and campus map are on top. Your first class is"—she rotated her wrist, checking her watch —"in about an hour. Good luck and welcome to FUCN'A."

"An hour!" Katz squeaked. "I thought I wasn't starting classes until Thursday."

The WANCer shrugged. "I don't make the schedule, Ms. Karak. Good luck," she said again in a clear dismissal.

Aren't I supposed to have a guided tour of the campus? Shoot— that was yesterday!

She swallowed the rising panic as she strode back toward the outer door and shoved it open.

Breathe. Calm. Think.

She spotted a bench tucked under a majestic tree and headed toward it. Setting her oversized purse on the bench, she dropped down next to it and tore the top of the envelope open.

Best get started.

Schedule first.

She glanced at her watch and then searched for a pen from her bag.

First things first.

She did indeed have a class in an hour. Leafing through the pages, she got herself calibrated as to what her next steps were then matched the schedule and classrooms to the map.

I can do this.

Just like arriving late to a business conference with presentations to slam. The only difference was the audience. Instead of pinch-faced magnates set in their ways, she'd be facing open-minded shifters from all backgrounds with the single goal of being the best FUC agent they could be.

And it's my job to help them do that.

First lesson. Adaptability. In any situation.

Including this one.

With another glance at her watch and the map, she stood and slung her bag over her shoulder. Time to go.

Whatever other prep work needed to be done would be done mentally on the way then on the fly once class started.

I can do this.

I have to do this.

Now I understand the pressure Darcy was talking about.

Except, this time, Katz was instructing, whereas Darcy had been learning.

If Darcy can do this, so can I.

Mother won't win on this.

I'll prove I can succeed at whatever I choose to do, without her support.

"Remember to use your opponents' momentum. Yes, that's right. Just like that, Lydia," Zeek LeBrute said before turning to observe the next student's stance in the training facility on the FUCN'A campus.

"Squirt," he said, looking down.

"King Kong Junior."

Zeek grinned.

Bryah Lam grinned back.

"How are the flying lessons coming along?" he asked, adjusting the height of her loose fist and pushing her foot into the proper distance.

Bryah shrugged, allowing Zeek to adjust her stance. "Smooth. Instructor Columba and I only have a few more sessions before she heads back to ASS."

"Is she taking Joe Suricatta with her when she goes back to the Avian Soaring Society? He unnerves me."

Bryah laughed. "No idea. But he unnerves everyone. Don't worry about it." She swung her arm, fist connecting with an easy block.

"Better. Harder next time," Zeek said. "Punch like you mean it."

"Didn't want to hurt you."

Zeek scoffed but grinned at Bryah. She was the best friend of his cousin, Corra Terry, and girlfriend of Corra's brother, Caleb Terry.

Her foot snapped up toward his chin.

"Angle is wrong."

"How do you like working here?" she asked before her foot came up again.

"Better. It's good. Not what I expected. I'm still amazed they accepted my proposal after everything that happened."

Bryah shrugged. "Guess they see your potential. You

proved that you're not like your dad and grandfather," she said, referring to incidents involving his cousin Corra last fall. "How are the renovations coming along at the family estate?"

"Try the next combination of strikes," he instructed, repositioning himself for her attack. "Great, since Mom took over. The new gyms look fantastic. It'll be great running legit businesses now. We're hoping to start interviewing for new hires soon."

"Awesome. You should have a party or something. Maybe you can get Darcy's sister to help with that. I think that's her thing—make it all sophisticated and stuff. Whoops! Are you okay?"

She stared, wide-eyed; her strike had connected unexpectedly.

Zeek's ears rang as his pulse tripped. He nodded and chuckled. "Lucky hit while I was distracted."

Bryah's eyes narrowed on him.

He could see the clockworks ticking behind her assessing gaze. "Yeah, I'll keep that in mind. Keep up the good work," he said, moving on to the next student.

"You're coming to The Hub tonight, right?"

"Maybe," he said as he assessed Vo's stance. It was perfect, so he just clapped him on the back and moved on, putting more distance between himself and the too-curious and observant squirrel shifter his cousin was dating.

He cursed under his breath.

She'd caught him off guard with the mention of Darcy Karak's sister.

Katherine Karak. Katz.

Distant acquaintance—very distant—as far as the world knew.

Sophisticated was the perfect word to describe the beautiful feline shifter that his gorilla-self seemed to take an interest in.

So much so he'd wanted to beat his chest in territorial declaration when they'd met all those months ago.

Focus, Zeek.

Shaking off the surprise mention, he got his head back into the job at hand: Instructing FUCN'A cadets in the finer points of whole-body martial arts in human form—in this class. There was also one for augmented fighting techniques in shifter form. And a "blending in with the shadier sector of human populations" role-play class.

Street smarts.

He glanced at Bryah again. Something that she and Corra were already well adapted for.

However, many of the other students were from middle- and upper-class backgrounds and had no notion what happened below the third floor, let alone in trailer parks or inner-city zones where the street sweepers couldn't reach.

The underbelly of society that agents might have to mingle with.

Zeek's specialty, as well as fighting dirty when necessary.

A world he'd left behind, with Caleb's encouragement, but he couldn't argue that certain skills were useful.

And the Furry United Coalition Newbie Academy agreed. Whatever skills their agents might need to keep them alive in sticky situations were valuable assets.

And Daniel "Zeek" LeBrute had a résumé to build if he wanted his business to be legit.

He was no longer his father's lackey or his grandfather's thug.

He shoved the twinge of guilt aside as he dodged a student's fist. His grandfather and his father, Rollo, were riding cots behind bars.

Because Zeek had turned on them. His family.

For his cousins.

And for Katz.

He instructed the last student then clasped his hands behind his back and walked back the length of the Academy training gym, assessing.

His old life had ended last autumn.

FUCN'A had given him a chance at something new.

He drew a deep breath and expelled the lingering guilt.

It was time to build a new concept of what family was to him.

Which started with his mother and his cousins, Caleb and Corra Terry.

And the Furry United Coalition Newbie Academy.

2

"In our next class, we'll identify the different tiers of shifter hierarchy and why you need to know them," Katz said in closing, releasing the cadets from the session.

Group noise filled the classroom as they rose from their chairs and collected their belongings to move to their next class.

"That was great, Katz," Corra Terry, her brother's girlfriend, said while approaching her. "I had no idea how complex life is for the one-percent. So many rules."

Katz shrugged. "It's silly, really. A holdover from the old days."

"A way to separate the masses, huh? The sparklies from the grubs like us."

"Grubs." Katz snorted in a very unsophisticated way and rolled her eyes. "It's all just pretense. But it's vital for infiltration."

"Yeah, I know." Corra smiled and shouldered her. "You're coming to The Hub tonight, right?"

Kats smiled at the intimate gesture. She'd grown to really like Corra since she'd stood up to Darcy and Katz' mother when their parents were trying to force him into an arranged marriage for the sake of the family company.

Which they did for all of their children to maintain the dynasty.

Katz was next and last in line. It was part of the argument she'd had with her mother.

Katherine was expected to toe the family line as she'd promised.

She sighed.

"The Hub? Oh, right, the pub in town your friend Bryah works at. She makes amazing French 75's, by the way. I haven't had one as good as that since the last time I was in town."

"Yes, she has quite the talent for alcoholic beverages. So, you'll be there, right?"

"To be honest, Corra, Mother held me up and I barely made it here in time. I have a lot of paperwork to review and class planning to do before tomorrow. I was barely holding on by my claw tips today. And I haven't napped yet."

"Nah, you did great. I have to get going to another class, but we'll talk later at The Hub. Oh hey, Miranda!" Corra called out on her way through the door.

Katz glanced to the open door as Miranda Brownsmith, a top FUC agent and occasional fill-in FUCN'A director—not to mention fierce sabretooth-bunny shifter—entered the room, bouncing.

Katz blinked, trying to adjust her focus on the famous bunny shifter. "Hello, Agent Brownsmith."

"I'll call you Katherine, and you call me Miranda."

"Katz."

Miranda nodded and smiled. "Ready for the campus tour you missed yesterday?"

"Of course." Katz shoved her papers into her bag and slung it over her shoulder. "I apologize for arriving late."

"You're here now," Miranda said, leading the way through

the building. She pointed out all the key locations Katz recalled from the map, at a speed that felt more like power walking than a leisure tour.

Through the education facility, the sports facilities and grounds, the student dormitories, and staff housing, and back through administration and various leisure buildings.

The place was better than some of the five-star resorts she'd been to in her lifetime, minus the access to alcohol at all hours of the day and night. Miranda chattered on about the function of every sector, including rules and regulations.

They bypassed a group of female cadets gushing about one of their instructors.

"...hot."

"...great butt!"

"...bet his hair is soft."

"And his hands! Have you noticed the size of his hands?"

"You know what they say about big hands... Oh hey, Agent Brownsmith!" one said to Miranda, turning several shades of pink.

She greeted them, ignoring the comments.

Katz followed Miranda, who'd resumed walking.

"Who were they talking about?" she asked, curiosity piqued.

"Hmm? Oh, our martial arts instructor. He hasn't been here very long. I'm sure you know him— Oh wait, there he is." She gestured across the open green space where more female students clustered around a blond man that towered above the crowd.

Katz' heart hammered in her chest. Her mouth went dry.

Jealousy roared its way up her throat, but she caught herself in time, dispelling it with a dainty clearing of her throat. Throat tight, she said, "Oh, yes, he's familiar. Related to the Terrys, isn't he?" Her voice sounded strangely high in her effort to portray mild interest.

His long blond hair was pulled back from his face. Gone

were the leather jacket, jeans, and boots. He wore a shirt, tie, and slacks with shiny loafers. Despite the drastic change of appearance, Katz recognized her former gorilla lover.

His size and build were unmistakable.

Miranda glanced at her, a slow grin lighting her face. She bounced on the balls of her feet, though her expression turned thoughtful. "Their cousin."

Katz felt exposed. Her heart hammered harder.

It's just...surprise. It doesn't matter if he's here. It doesn't change anything.

But he cleans up so well!

I'm here to focus on my work. Not drool over a super-hot gorilla shifter that knows how to—

"Katz? Katherine Karak? What are you doing here?" His voice boomed across the open space as he barreled toward her.

Miranda adjusted her direction, leading Katz straight toward Zeek and his cluster of students. All female. With glistening eyes.

The area reeked of hormones.

Were they licking their lips?

Jealousy twitched through her. She swallowed a building hiss.

She bowed her head, tucking a long dark curl behind her ear as she wrangled her baser instinct into a tidy little glass box and shoved it into a dark hole in her heart.

No, she vowed.

Back under control, she lifted her head and met Zeek's wide, soulful gray eyes.

The students had turned toward her with curious stares.

Miranda clapped her hands together. "This is Instructor Karak. She's here to teach some of our social etiquette classes for a couple of semesters," she said to the students.

Katz mustered her brightest smile.

"And we have a special project lined up for her to work on with Instructor LeBrute."

Zeek gaped at Miranda.

Katz' smile froze. "Excuse me, what?" she asked through her clenched teeth.

This time Zeek had made it as far as the campus green before the students descended on him. They surrounded him with questions about the course, about his experience, about himself.

He stood paralyzed as they closed in, unable to ignore their appreciative glances, seductive body posturing, and sweeping caresses along his arms, shoulders, and back.

"Hey!" he yelped when someone's hands brushed his ass.

Someone giggled. "Oops, sorry."

Exasperated, he glanced up to see Miranda Brownsmith approaching from the far side.

Relief flooded him in hopes she'd rescue him.

His gaze took in the woman next to her, and his heart stopped then began an all-out gorilla thump.

Katz!

He hadn't realized he'd shouted until all the young women around him spun to look in her direction. They moved aside to allow Agent Brownsmith room to approach and introduce Katz as a new instructor.

New instructor?

A special project?

He blinked, focusing on what Miranda was saying.

"...about ends the tour, Katz. We're happy to have you join our staff, and if you need anything, just ask," Miranda said to Katz as she started to bounce away.

"Wait, which way is it back to housing?" Katz called after her.

"Zeek, you're going that way, right? He can take you there." Miranda grinned and was gone in a flash.

"Damn," Katz muttered, not meeting Zeek's eyes. Instead, she turned to look in each direction of the green space to figure out which way to go.

Zeek didn't move.

The students began to disperse, casting furtive glances at Katz.

Zeek ignored them. "Housing is back this way." He gestured across the green, pulling her attention.

The last student drifted away toward the dorms.

Katz glanced at him, turning in the direction he'd indicated and began walking at a pace that didn't suit the spiked heels she wore. "Thank you," she threw over her shoulder as an afterthought.

"Wait," he called, jogging forward to catch up to her. "I'm heading that way."

She threw him another glance and a wan smile but maintained her awkward pace.

"I missed you," he said.

Her heel dragged, and she stumbled.

His hand shot out and caught her against him.

She quickly straightened herself, brushed the hair from her face, and said, "Thanks. Again." And resumed walking, with a limp.

"You're hurt," Zeek said, swinging her up into his arms, cradling her against his chest.

"Zeek! Put me down. I'm fine!" Horror filled her expression. "Put me down before anyone sees me like this," she demanded, her eyes darting around for witnesses.

But Zeek's gorilla liked having his kitten close to his chest. He pulled her in closer.

"Zeek," she tried again with a huff. "This is highly inappropriate."

"You're hurt. I'll help you get back to your place. Which one is it?"

"I can walk. This is my first day, and it's had a crap start, and this is not helping."

He looked down into her stubborn face. Beautiful face. The color in her cheeks flamed.

Angry face.

He carefully set her back on her feet but refused to release her hand, draping it over his forearm for support.

She sighed but seemed content to at least be back on her feet. She didn't say anything more until they reached her house. "This one."

He grinned. "I'm just over there. We're neighbors." He pointed across the path and one over from hers.

Her eyes darted to his house, to his face, then back to the house. She opened her mouth to speak, but Zeek cut in.

"Want to have dinner tonight? We can catch up."

"You cook?" she blurted out.

"Yeah, of course I cook. I love cooking. Do you like food? I guess I've never asked you that before since we were so busy… you know." Blissful memories of their days and nights engaged in passionate lovemaking filled his brain.

"I mean, I…uhm… have plans. Corra Terry asked me to go to the Hub tonight." She dropped her gaze at his words. Then her cheeks flamed, eyes darting back up to his face.

He looked down.

Oh. His memories of their time together were a little obvious. He'd gone hard.

"That won't be happening anymore, Zeek. It seems we're work colleagues now, and it would be highly inappropriate," she said, lifting her chin.

She was so cute when she did that.

15

But then, she ruined the effect when her eyes dropped again and her tongue darted out between her lips.

He hardened even more so that it was bordering on painful.

The scent of her desire drifted on the breeze surrounding them.

The urge to chest-thump returned.

He just wanted to kiss those plump little lips and taste that pink little tongue.

No longer thinking, he reached for her, her face small between his hands. She stared at him as though mesmerized.

His pulse pounded through him. Through his heart, in his ears, down to his dick. But mostly in his heart.

"I've missed my little kitten," he breathed against her mouth as his lips closed over hers in the gentlest of kisses.

She melted into him, her hands splayed against his chest, her mouth opened to the sweep of his tongue.

He was sure he heard her purring.

A sharp pain broke the spell.

"Ow!" He jerked back, bringing a finger to his lip.

"I said that won't happen anymore. And I'm not a—your little kitten." She scowled at him.

"But you were purring!"

"I was not." She straightened, pushing her hair over her shoulder.

"Katz, I know your purr. And I know all the things that make you purr."

"Stop that!" she hissed, eyes darting up and down the path. "Someone might hear you."

"So?"

She huffed, spun on her good foot, and limped her way to her front door. Within the safety of the doorway, she remembered her manners and turned back toward Zeek. "Thank you for your assistance, Instructor LeBrute. Perhaps we can meet in the cafeteria tomorrow to discuss whatever this project is."

Or you can spend the night and we can talk in bed...

Her stubborn expression told him that wasn't going to happen. Tonight. "As you wish."

She frowned, eyes narrowed.

Something poked at his gut. Was that guilt?

She'd said no, and he'd kissed her anyway.

He dipped his head, contrite. "I'll see you around," he mumbled and wandered home.

3

The afternoon's moments with Zeek replayed through Katz' mind on a continuous loop.

Since she'd arrived so late, she hadn't had the time to unpack and settle in. With the excess energy from her unnerving reunion with Zeek fizzling through her, it didn't take long to finish the task.

Once she turned her attention to the paperwork and the class planning, though, the excess energy did her little good when it came to focus.

She even tried pacing while reading, which proved to be useless.

No longer able to see the print through the memories of the sensation of Zeek's arms around her, his scent, and his kiss, work was impossible.

She growled her frustration, slapping the sheets of typed papers against her thighs then tossing them onto the table.

This was exactly why she'd given him up in the first place all those months ago. When he was around, he was all she could think about.

What blissful weeks they'd had together!

She sighed, her cheeks flushed as her pulse raced.

"Stop it, Katherine Karak! You broke things off for a reason."

Liar.

You never actually broke things off, did you? You ghosted the gorgeous gorilla and ran away.

Back to your parents.

"Oh my god, I'm so lame! Lame!" she screamed to the empty room.

A moment later, there was a knock on the door. "Are you okay in there?"

Shit.

She whipped the door open. "Yes I'm fine, just practicing some stuff. No worries." She grinned.

The neighbor's eyes shifted right then left in confusion. "Oh. Okay, alrighty then. Let me know if you need anything. I'm Floyd. Floyd Marmotte."

"Nice to meet you, Floyd. I'm Katz." She gave him a little smile and a wave then shut the door.

"I have to get out of here. Less than a day and I'm already stir-crazy." She glanced at her Alhambra watch.

Hadn't Corra said they were meeting at The Hub in town tonight?

"I could really use one of those perfect French 75's that— what's her name? Bryah? Yes, Bryah, makes."

Having decided, she grabbed her oversized purse from where she'd tossed it onto the couch, found shoes with lower heels, snatched her keys from the wall hook, and headed for her car.

Once she got there, she stared at the keys in her hand.

What if one French 75 wasn't enough?

Zeek wandered through her mind again.

"I might need three to purge him so I can sleep tonight."

"Pardon?" A passerby stopped.

"Uhm." She thought. "Uhm, do you know how to get to The Hub from here?"

He waved toward the highway. "Road takes you straight into town. Can't miss it. But if you want to run it, there's a well-worn trail. Can't miss that either." He gestured toward a break in the trees just beyond the edge of the compound.

"Thanks. I'm Katz, by the way." She held out a hand to shake.

"Joe Suricatta."

She squinted at the thin man with the narrow bearded face and glasses. "I think we may have met."

"We have. Goodnight," he said and continued on his way.

She stared after him a moment, shrugged, and decided running was the best option. Glancing around, she removed her shoes and dropped them, along with her keys, into her purse while running toward the tree break.

Ensuring she was alone once she'd made the shadows of the tree line, she stripped off the rest of her clothes, folded them neatly, and placed them into her purse atop her shoes then shifted.

She stretched, elongating her furry brown forelegs, flexing her paws, then did the same with her hindquarters till her spine was loose. She gingerly clasped the expensive purse between her teeth, head held high, and began trotting along the path, which was far clearer in the dark with her feline sight.

The size of the bag made it difficult to run full-out, so she contented herself with a steady trot through the forest.

She sighted the back of the familiar property. The Hub shared a lot with a motel run by Old Carl. Forcefully ignoring the motel, she dropped her bag next to a cluster of bushes.

Ignore the hotel. Ignore the hotel.

More memories of her and Zeek together tumbled through her brain.

She squeezed her eyes shut and shifted back into her human form.

Reaching for her clothes, she froze at the sound of a deep voice.

"You came."

Uhm. Her gaze darted from shadow to shadow this side of the tree line. She snatched her purse back up to her chest, trying to cover herself.

Zeek?

He emerged from another cluster of bushes about ten feet away.

Her gaze traveled from his bare feet up the long legs, open fly, and dangling belt to the naked belly button and ripped abs.

She dry-swallowed, forcing her gaze to keep traveling up to his face and not stall on his glorious torso. Her hands gripped the handle of her bag tighter.

Not because she feared dropping it.

She feared throwing it away to reach for him to fondle all that muscled beauty. Like she used to. Months and months ago.

She closed her eyes.

"Katz? You okay? Need some help with your clothes?"

"No. I can handle it. You go on and put your shirt on. And go away."

"Go away?"

"Err, go on inside."

"But I don't mind—"

"Go. Zeek. Now," she rasped out, opening her eyes.

The corner of his lips lifted. "Yes, ma'am." He sauntered away at a leisurely pace.

"Jerk," she muttered.

His low laughter floated back to her on the breeze.

She dressed as fast as possible and rushed to the door like she was being chased.

Just in case he was still outside. By now, she'd come to the realization she couldn't trust herself to be alone with him.

As much as she told herself she had plans—a new life as a solo, independent woman—her desire for him was still vivid and magnetic.

This was bad. Very bad.

Why did he have to be here?

This was her chance to prove to her parents, herself too, that she could forge her own path and prove her independence. Like Darcy had.

And this infatuation with Zeek was just going to ruin everything.

No. It wasn't. Because she was not going to give in to her puss—kitty. Her kitty.

She ripped the front door open and stalked inside.

Flicking her hair back over her shoulder, she tilted her nose up and sauntered toward the bar and settled on a stool, purse on her lap.

The petite brunette popped up from behind the bar, eyes alight with a wide smile. "Katz! I'll get your French 75 in a jiff."

Katz sighed. Relieved. Something was going to be perfect. Even if this first day was a disaster.

"Where's Corra? She said she'd be here."

Bryah pulled a face. "Got held up with some last-minute assignment."

"Somersby, please." Zeek's gravelly voice rippled right up her spine as he settled onto the stool beside her.

Fuck.

———

"We should talk," Zeek said to Katz, ignoring her attempt to ignore him.

She sat straighter on the barstool, still staring forward. Bryah placed Katz' French 75 in front of her.

Katz's fingers slid across the worn wood to caress the base of the glass and up the stem to the bowl and lifted the drink to her perfect lips.

She sipped, closed her eyes, and sighed.

Should I bring up the past?

She had dropped off the face of the earth, and she was still avoiding him.

He'd come to terms with it, once he'd got his gorilla under control after their surprise meeting in the green space.

He could be aloof too. Even though his desire for her hadn't gone anywhere.

"You don't have to talk. You can listen." He didn't turn toward her but kept his voice low so that only she would hear. "You ghosted me."

She cringed but didn't acknowledge the comment.

He went on. "We had a real good time together. Hours... days locked away in hotel rooms. A real good time." His voice dropped lower.

She adjusted her posture on her seat.

"Whatever your reason was for disappearing without a word... I guess that's your business. I certainly never expected you to show up here of all places. Anywhere in the world you could have gone and you come back here. *Here.*"

She threw back the rest of her drink with a single gulp and asked Bryah for another. "You didn't text me either, Zeek."

He sipped his cider and placed it back on the bar, letting his thick fingers slide up and down the sweating glass.

She watched his hands from the corner of her eye. The color in her cheeks turned peachy as she licked her lips.

He chuckled.

Her eyes darted back to the wall of bottles behind the bar.

Katz maintained her silence all the way through the first

half of her second drink. Then she turned on him, cheeks blazing, eyes sparkling like cut gold-green crystal.

Gold sparks when she was angry or irritated and glittering emerald when she was aroused.

Tonight, they seemed to be a blend of both.

"I'm just an independent working woman," she said.

"Okay."

"Minding my own business. Making my way. Standing on my own two feet."

"Right."

"Me…" She wavered, thumb pointed at herself. "All by myself."

Two more sips and she'd be slurring. By the bottom of the glass, she'd be stumbling.

She swiped her glass for another gulp. "So good," she whispered, her expression one of bliss.

She held up a finger. "If Darshy can do it, I can do it."

"If Darcy can do what?"

"Eshcape my mother'zh clawsh." She turned back toward Bryah. "Bree-ah, this drink is fabuloush. Another pleash."

Bryah's wide gaze darted between Zeek and Katz, who leaned dangerously backward on her stool to help gravity release every drop left in the glass.

"It seems she doesn't do well with liquor," Zeek said.

Bryah patted Katz' hand. "Give me an hour and I'll see if I can find you another one."

Katz squinted at her watch. She turned on Zeek with a scowl.

"You weren't shupposed to be here. You were supposed to be tucked away at your place doing other thingsh. Not here. You're a fighter. Not a teasher," she accused.

"Things change," he said with a shrug.

"You…" She licked her lips. "You don't wear ties and loaf —loaferzh."

He waited, seeing where she was going with this. Unease wriggled in his gut.

No. Ties and loafers weren't his deal.

But he wasn't about to tell her that it was her fault he'd decided to do it.

"Are you a bad boy gone good?" She arched a brow.

He laughed. "Is that even possible? With my history?" he asked, taking a swig from his drink.

It was rhetorical, of course.

"Of course it is. Don't be shilly." She waved a hand. "You have a heart of gold, and your loyalty may have been misplaced, but pfffsh, whatever. All of that shtuff's in the past. I start new. You start new, too." She leaned close to him, smiling.

God, she was adorable when she was drunk.

And passionate.

He surveyed the bar. Mostly locals—humans, truckers, loggers, hippies clinging to the last century. But it wouldn't be long before she invited one of them out for a night of fun.

He'd rather it were him, but he knew she'd regret it if it were any of these guys.

"I think we need to get you home, Katz."

She grinned, licking her lips.

Zeek pulled his wallet from his pocket, dropping bills on the bar for the drinks, and reached for Katz' purse. To Bryah he said, "I'm going to help Ms. Karak home safely."

Her eyes flicked between the two again. She nodded. "Thanks, Zeek. Oh hey, I almost forgot. Caleb said he's coming home tomorrow."

He nodded. "Ma will want to have dinner. I'll call her."

She grinned. "Give Sheila my best. I'll see you on campus tomorrow." Leaning down, she reached below the bar, pulled up a bottle of water, and handed it to Zeek. "Make sure she hydrates. I haven't seen anyone slide under the liquor that fast in a while."

Katz reached for it and pulled it in tight to her chest. "Thank you, sweetie."

Zeek steered Katz out of The Hub and walked her back toward the dark path. He glanced at the hotel.

Too many memories there. Best get her home.

She giggled, broke free of his grip, and headed toward the hotel office. "I'll bet Old Carl still has my card on file."

"Not tonight, sweetheart."

She ignored him, still headed for the office in a crooked line.

Ensuring there were no witnesses, he guided her back toward the shadows then, as quickly as possible, stripped and stashed his clothes in her giant purse.

"Oh, Zeek," she breathed, staring at him with wide eyes. "You're so beautiful."

Her eyes slid all over his bare flesh, making it obvious he could feel her gaze on him.

She grinned when her gaze stopped at his hips. "There it is." She licked her lips again.

I really wish she wouldn't do that.

He sighed, shifted into his gorilla, and crouched.

She squealed as he threw her over his shoulder, ass up and squirming. "What are you doing? The hotel isn't far. I can walk."

He grunted then secured one hand over her ass to hold her in place while he used the other to run back to campus through the woods.

She bounced and complained all the while, periodically beating on his back to be let down.

And he'd periodically slap her ass with his free hand to encourage her to stop.

And maybe just because it was a good excuse to slap her ass again.

No one was on the path between the houses when he

stopped outside her house. He set her on her feet, and she wavered, catching her balance after all the upside down bumping and slapping. She seemed unable to coordinate enough to get the key in the door, so Zeek was forced to shift back.

It was faster than trying to manipulate the small key with his gorilla fingers.

Just as the door swung open, her hand slapped his bare ass with a loud smack, followed by a body slam, shoving him into the house.

He managed to turn and shove the door closed as she shuffled him backward to the couch, growling all the while. His legs hit the end of the couch, and she went over with him, landing sprawled across the length of his body.

This wasn't quite how he expected the night to go.

Honestly, he thought he was going to have a chat with her to lay down some rules, like she stay on her side of the campus and he stay on his.

Until he figured things out.

Simple.

Except they lived across the path from each other. They'd have to work on Miranda's project together.

And he was currently naked on her couch and she was draped on top of him.

So much for rules. But he hadn't actually laid them down—yet.

However, as much as his gorilla missed his kitty, and his dick was raring for another round of trapped-naked-survivor, his heart was packing his bag and heading for the road.

Zeek had plans of his own.

Time to go.

Just as she stopped mauling him, she slumped and a loud snore erupted, vibrating against his chest.

He sighed.

Reluctant to move her, he relaxed under her dead weight for a while, reveling in the feel of her body against his.

I've missed this.

Her silky hair spread out from her head and fanned out over his chest and neck. Inhaling deeply, he reacquainted himself with her unique bouquet mixed with her peony perfume.

No one knew.

No one but the two of them knew about those blissful days they'd spent in each other's arms. What started out as a hookup the very first night she'd set foot in The Hub for the first time had turned into something else altogether. Then, when he'd traveled to California on his grandfather's orders in pursuit of her brother and his cousin, they'd reunited, deepening an experience he'd never had before.

And in those moments, in his grandfather's study, when he'd given Zeek the order to get rid of her?

He'd made his choice, which had altered everything.

And she'd left. Without a word.

It was for the best.

I'm not good enough for her, anyway.

No matter what his gorilla or his heart said, they didn't belong together. That was why he had never tried to contact her either.

In fact, he'd deleted her number from his phone to avoid the temptation.

And now, temptation was spread all over his naked body, testing his will.

4

The sound of hissing water roused Katz to consciousness.

Eyes closed, the backs of her eyelids were illuminated peach shades as she honed in on her senses.

Is something leaking?

Her eyes popped open. She floated on a wave of disorientation, trying to understand where she was, as the sound of running water persisted.

She bolted upright into a sitting position, blinded by sunlight streaming in through the large living room window. Her flesh prickled under the chill of the air, her covering crumpled in her lap, seated on the couch as she was.

She was in her bra. Peeking under the sheet, she determined she also wore her panties.

It required another thirty seconds to absorb the other details of the room around her. Not her apartment. It was her temporary home at the Academy. She sighed.

Right.

Getting to her feet, she padded around on bare feet to determine the source of the running water. Not the kitchen faucet or pipes below.

Her clothing and shoes were at the end of the couch.

Following the sound to its source, steam billowed out of the master bedroom ensuite.

She gulped, glancing down at her minimal attire.

The Hub. French 75's. Two?

Oh, Katz, what did you do this time?

She froze, staring at the bathroom door.

Please don't let it be a trucker, please don't let it be a trucker...

Spying her bathrobe abandoned on the foot of the bed, she shrugged into it, knotting the belt as tight as possible.

The bed was undisturbed.

Whatever had happened, it had happened in the living room.

She swallowed.

It was like an accident scene. You didn't want to look at the gruesome details that might scar you for life, but you couldn't not, either.

A shower was a good sign, right? Whoever it was, they enjoyed cleanliness.

But, it was also a sign they were washing away evidence of...

"Zeek?"

Oh no. Her mouth dropped open.

"Oh hey, you're up," he said, stepping out of the bathroom, hair dripping, torso gleaming, abs shimmering in the golden morning light, and a towel fetchingly low on his hips.

Her heart pounded in her ears.

This is so much worse than a trucker.

"I said this wasn't going to happen anymore," she spat, guilt flaring into anger.

"Nothing hap—"

"You took advantage of me, didn't you?"

"Uh, no. In fact, you—"

"Don't try to turn this on me."

Hands on hips, hair still wet, skin still gleaming, he frowned. Then deliberately turned away from Katz, reaching for his clothes, set neatly on the night table.

Nostrils flared in his annoyance, he pulled the towel off and tossed it at her then reached for his clothes.

She spun around, cheeks flaming.

"Nothing happened. You got drunk. I had to run you home. You sprawled on me—on the couch. Snoring. All damned night. As soon as I was able to get out from under you, I slept on the chair to make sure you were okay. I woke about ten minutes ago and decided to grab a quick shower. Then go home."

She spun back toward him. "And why am I undressed?" She snapped, hands on hips.

"I remembered you don't like your clothes wrinkled."

She huffed.

As soon as she heard his zipper slide into place, she spun back to him, ready with more, but she paused, seeing his set mouth.

He was pulling his socks on now.

He's annoyed.

At me.

She swallowed whatever she was going to say.

His left brow rose as he regarded her.

"Thank you," she said.

I'm sorry. I missed you. I-I care about you.

"I'll see you around campus," he said, pulling his shirt on. "I'm going to try to find out what this project is that Miranda has for us." The line of his lips didn't ease as he pulled his boots on. "She's already jogged by four times. I think I can catch her on the next loop."

He straightened, leveled his gaze on her—his soulful gaze— then left without another word.

I can't. I can't. I can't.

31

"Thanks," she whispered again to the empty house after the front door clicked shut.

Mentally shaking herself, she glanced at the clock by the bed.

Crapolla!

She ran for the shower.

Zeek shoved thoughts of Katz's warm, supple, curvy body from his mind.

She was very clear that they wouldn't be resuming their affair, and she was also very clear she didn't want to acknowledge it had ever happened.

His chest tightened. He clenched his jaw.

You know you don't deserve her anyway.

He glanced down at the loafers and slacks he'd swapped out for after lunch before the classroom session. Mornings were for martial arts training classes, afternoons for traditional classroom teaching.

I look ridiculous dressed like this.

What was I thinking? I'll never fit into her world. I'm always going to be just a thug.

He sighed.

Stop. Mindset. Things are different now.

Are they, though?

Yes, shut up.

He'd even bought a bag to carry his instructor stuff. He'd learned that professionals carried leather satchels.

He checked his father Rollo's voice at the door before it could rant about manly-men and looking like an idiot with a man-purse. Rollo was the idiot. Someone Zeek decided he'd never be like.

Honestly? He liked the bag.

He was standing in the classroom admiring his investment when the door opened and Miranda bounced in, followed by Katz.

"Nice bag," Katz said. "My older brother has one like that in black. The brown suits you."

Zeek smiled at the compliment.

"Okay, right to business. I have another meeting in five minutes," Miranda cut in. "Zeek, you've been teaching martial arts and have a lifetime of experience with the underworld—the part of the world most people don't get to see. Katz, you're here to teach our students how to mingle with the upper echelon of society, the one-percenters."

She bounced on the balls of her feet, looking from Zeek to Katz and back again. "It's fortuitous that you're both at the Academy at the same time. I want you to run a class that combines a common skill set so that our cadets can navigate both worlds whenever they need to. Questions?"

"But I can't—"

"Why do we—"

"No? Perfect. Good luck!" Miranda bounced out the door in a blink, leaving them gaping in her wake.

Katz' shoulders slumped.

Zeek blew out a breath.

They looked at each other.

"We can do this," Zeek said.

"Of course, we can," Katz agreed, tossing a curl over her shoulder. "Just follow my lead."

"Your lead? You should follow mine. I've been instructing here longer, and the students know me better."

"I have more experience with presentations."

"And I'm better at winging it."

She snorted. "It's okay, Zeek. I'll lead and you stand by looking good. That's what the female students are here for anyway."

Stung, he jerked back a step. "What's that supposed to mean?"

She shrugged and strode toward the door. "Nothing. My class is starting. Let's meet this evening in the lounge to draft a plan."

"Can't. I have plans. Ma's making dinner for Caleb tonight."

She paused at the door with a frown. "Caleb's back? Aren't he and Darcy out in the field working a mission?"

"They're coming back for a few days."

Katz pulled her phone from her purse, scrolling. Her frown deepened. "He hasn't messaged me. Whatever. Tomorrow morning then."

"Can't. I have my early morning regimen followed by martial arts class."

"Well, when can you manage?" she snapped. "Send me a calendar invitation for when you're available."

Dropping her phone back into her purse, she disappeared.

Zeek sighed then turned back to his stuff set on the desk.

She likes my bag.

He grinned.

5

Katz was still grumbling on her way back to her place after classes finished.

It was just like Darcy to not tell her what was going on with him.

She'd emailed him the details of her tenure at the Academy, along with her travel itinerary, so that they could meet up when he was finished with his mission.

He probably didn't even open my email.

She sighed, dropping her purse on the table inside the front door.

"Heya, sis! Nice place."

Katz' heart leapt into her throat as she froze in place.

She rounded the corner to find Darcy splayed on a comfy chair by the front window.

"Isis almighty, Darcy! Don't do that!" She rushed over and slapped his shoulder. "You're going to give me a heart attack one of these days."

He grinned, mischief glinting in his gold-green eyes. "I'll stop when you're actually old enough for that threat to hold any weight."

She scowled at him. "Why didn't you tell me you were coming?"

"I wanted to surprise you. Like you surprised me with your visit and news that Mom and Dad wanted me to get married. Remember?"

Her gaze honed in on his face. "What's going on? What do you want? Are they here? Are they leaning on you to pressure me to go back? I just got here, and I'm not going back yet."

"Whoa!" he said, laughing. "No, I haven't been in touch with them recently. Wow, someone—you—is edgy." He grinned at her.

"Stop grinning at me," she snarled.

"Mom and Dad are on *your* case now, huh?"

Katz flopped onto the sofa. "I'd say you have no idea, but I know you do."

She relayed the spat she had with their mother that caused her delay in arriving at the Academy and thus her unimpressive first day.

"Just forget about it. You'll adjust. Relax."

How can I? Zeek is here.

She stared at her brother until those errant thoughts slid by.

Watching her face, his expression turned sympathetic. "Look, just let Mom and Dad slide away. Focus on you, and day by day, you'll blossom into more than you are."

She studied him, allowing herself to relax a little. "That's really sweet of you to say, Darcy."

"Hey, that's what big brothers are for. Got any snacks? Caleb was too anxious to see Bryah and wouldn't let me stop for food on the drive here from the airport."

She blinked and laughed, rising from the couch to check the kitchen cupboards. "No idea. Let's go see." As she reached for the pantry door, her stomach growled. "Hey, want to get steak at that diner we met at last time? They had decent food."

Darcy moved up beside her to peer into the cupboard.

"Nah, I'm actually supposed to be having dinner at the Terry estate with Caleb and Corra." He straightened and studied her a moment. "You should come." He grabbed a box of cookies from the shelf, rummaged his hand inside it, and extracted several, popping one into his mouth. His eyes rolled with chocolate bliss.

"You can't invite me to someone else's dinner, Darcy. Thanks, but that's inappropriate." She laughed.

Darcy's phone chimed during the moments of mutual cookie crunching as they enjoyed the treats together like when they were kids.

It chimed a second time.

Katz' phone buzzed from her purse.

The siblings looked at each other, reflecting the other's worry.

Mom and Dad? Another sibling?

She rushed for her phone as Darcy extracted his.

"Corra and Caleb are messaging me. Their aunt Sheila wants me to bring you to dinner." He laughed. "Corra must have told her you're here too."

Katz pulled her phone from her bag and unlocked it.

Zeek.

Corra told Mom you're instructing at the Academy now. I told her we're working on a project. She wants you to come to dinner tonight.

Katz' gut clenched as she stared at the text.

He didn't say he wanted me there.

It would be rude to decline an invitation from Mrs. LeBrute.

"I met Sheila the night Corra's grandfather and Sheila's husband, Rollo, were arrested at the estate. Sweet Isis, what a night," she mumbled.

"She's a great lady. Very kind," Darcy said.

Katz turned to regard her brother. "You think I should go."

He shrugged. "I already said you should come before they invited you." His grin returned. "Besides, I remember how you looked at Zeek that night at The Hub when you first arrived. Made me shudder. He's changed a lot since then, but who knows, you might even hit it off."

Hit it off.

Heat flooded her cheeks first, then the rest of her body. That night, he'd looked like a scruffy nineties grunge star that just screamed at her bad girl bones to go with.

And she did.

Wow, did I ever.

"Are you all right? You're suddenly looking a little flushed." His expression was concerned with a hint of suspicion.

"Yes, I find Zeek handsome." She lightened her tone with a shrug. "You know how I am about meeting new people."

A genuine smile touched Darcy's lips as he put his arms around her for a brotherly hug. "Yes, I know how anxious you get. And you're also talented at faking it till you make it. You'll be great. She'll love you."

Katz chuckled. "She doesn't need to love me. I just don't want to embarrass anyone."

"Impossible," he declared with a squeeze then headed toward the front door. "Listen, Caleb and I are staying in the guest quarters while we're here so we can do some more background work on our case. Meet us in the parking lot in an hour. I'll see if Caleb and Bryah can ride with Zeek since you're coming along too. You can ride with Corra and me."

She smiled. "Thanks. I'll be there."

They drove for what seemed an eternity. In reality, it was more like an hour before they turned off the two-lane highway onto a winding private drive that went on for another while. She remained quiet in the backseat. Darcy and Corra's low conversation lulled her into a desperately needed semi-nap.

She recalled her last visit and how impressed she'd been by the family estate.

Too many things had gone so…awry…that night.

Finally, the paved serpentine drive arrived at an open gate, which she recalled had been closed and guarded on her last visit. Beyond the gate, the path continued on until it opened to encircle a large water fountain. The house folded around it. The mountains were a jagged wall behind the house, beyond the forest.

Darcy parked his sports car next to Zeek's truck, and they all got out. Corra led the way to the front door, which swung open as they reached the top step. A butler welcomed them inside with a warm smile and collected their coats and purses.

"Thanks, Mr. C.," Corra said to the butler.

"You seem quite at home here, now," Katz said to Corra.

Corra turned and smiled. "I've had time in the last few months to visit and get to know Aunt Sheila since she took the place over from the Old Man."

Katz nodded. The Old Man. Corra, Caleb, and Zeek's cantankerous, power-hungry grandfather.

She sniffed, recalling how she'd requested a meeting to negotiate. He'd basically ended the meeting with an order for her to be "taken care of." And not in the pleasant way. But what rankled her scruff more was the way he'd treated his grandchildren.

"It's okay, Katz. He isn't here and won't be for a very long time—if ever," Corra said in response to Katz' growling.

She stopped instantly. "Sorry, didn't realize. So rude of me."

Corra grinned, bumping her shoulder. "It's a reasonable response."

The contact seemed to calm her as they entered a sitting

room, where Sheila looked up with a bright smile from her place on the sofa with Bryah and Caleb. Zeek stood apart, looking out the window.

Darcy was right.

Zeek had changed a lot.

He no longer looked like the scruffy bad boy. He still preferred the boots, leather, and jeans, but he was healthier looking now.

Despite seeing him at the Hub and on campus, the difference here, in *this* place, was much more pronounced.

This was his home.

And yet, he was still ill at ease.

He turned from the window as they entered. His eyes found hers then swept her whole body. She felt overdressed in her sundress and heels. Everyone else wore jeans, except Darcy, who wore his customary tailored suit.

But Zeek's gaze made her feel naked at the same time.

"It's so nice to see you again, Katz. I've heard so many wonderful things about you," Sheila was saying as she approached, greeting Katz with a warm hug.

Katz' startled gaze darted from Sheila to Zeek, who shrugged.

Had he told his mother about them? Katz realized she had no idea how close their relationship was.

Sheila gave Katz a little squeeze then released her.

It made her feel…welcome.

The experience was nothing like her mother's hugs, which were stiff and brief. But Katz always appreciated the effort.

This hug reminded her of when she was a child and her grandmother would hug her like she was trying to make them into one person.

Her eyes prickled, and a small lump appeared in her throat.

She blinked away the encroaching feeling and drew a breath

to clear the little wave of guilt that rolled through her. She shouldn't be comparing her mother to anyone else's.

She loved her mother.

No matter how difficult the lioness was, she'd always done what she thought was best and tried to be nurturing—in her way.

Small talk followed for a little while longer before they moved into the dining room where the conversation turned to family business. Katz was surprised by how candid Sheila was. There was no sense of feeling analyzed or stalked. Just open, welcome and warm.

"Mrs. LeBrute—" Katz began.

"Terry. I've filed for divorce and reverted to my maiden name. But in any case, call me Sheila," the older woman said.

"Sheila, thank you for inviting me to dinner. This is lovely."

Sheila nodded, accepting the thanks. "We've managed to retain our cook. If I'd done the cooking, you wouldn't be thanking me."

Katz laughed at the good-natured comment, but she noted Zeek's frown as he regarded his mother.

"You've let more staff go," he said.

Sheila nodded. "All of the family accounts are still frozen, since they were in your grandfather's control." To Katz, she clarified, "After the Furry United Coalition arrested my father and husband, the family assets were frozen and still remain inaccessible. We're lucky to have the house." She sipped her water before going on. "I found the business proposal you gave to my father and have been trying to use it as a framework to keep things going. When you met with him to negotiate on Corra and Darcy's behalf, you had some great observations and suggestions. Do you mind if I ask you some questions about it and how I can continue to improve things?"

"Absolutely. We can start with your main goal—what you want to achieve and why then go from there," Katz said.

Sheila put her fork down. "We come from old stock but took a hard hit during the Great Depression. My grandfather started this fight business for his family to keep them fed. It grew from there. My father had his own ideas of how things should be run. I want to leave something good behind for future generations."

"Ma, none of us want this," Zeek said.

"Maybe not. But if any of you have children, there will be something for them and their children." She shrugged. "I also plan to set up an organization for shifter children in need. So if none of you have children, then what we do now can benefit them."

Katz swallowed the well of emotion that rose at Sheila's words. "Those are very generous motives. I'll put some thought into what you've said, and we can meet to develop a plan that suits your needs."

"How is the training going?" Caleb asked.

Zeek shrugged. "The fighters that were interested in legitimate fighting are training as hard as they always did. The ones that left…" He shrugged.

"Are probably making better money in the rings, especially now that the Old Man isn't retaining so much of the prize money for himself," Caleb said, "but they are still unregulated and illegal, and Darcy and I are working to shut them down."

Sheila nodded again. "Zeek's been keeping them fit until we can get all the paperwork in order to compete—make sure everything is done right. His work at the Academy for extra income helps finance everything."

"Zeek is a great teacher," Bryah interjected. "He's an awesome addition to the Academy, with his own flavor of skills."

"I appreciate you all vouching for me. I didn't think they'd take my proposal seriously, given my past."

"You earned it, Zeek. We've all seen how hard you worked

to overcome your addictions and help Aunt Sheila build the new business," Corra said, reaching out to touch her cousin's hand.

"I'm sure it hasn't been easy," Caleb said with an edge to his voice.

Zeek nodded but didn't comment. He picked up his glass, lifted it over the table, and cleared his throat.

Something tugged at Katz' heart.

When Zeek looked up, the emotion in his eyes was raw, but he smiled.

"To family and building something new," he said.

She lifted her glass along with everyone else, her gaze catching Darcy's with a smile.

Darcy's grin widened when he turned his attention to Corra over the rim of his glass as he sipped to Zeek's toast.

Corra nodded with a smile.

"I'd like to add to that sentiment," he said, standing, holding his glass toward Corra. "Last fall, Corra agreed to be my partner." They grinned at each other.

Katz recalled the promise ring he'd had her fetch from an antique shop to give to Corra. The lovely antique piece caught the soft light of the room.

Darcy went on, turning so that he looked down at Katz. "It's perfect that you're here too, Katz, to share the news with our closest people. Corra and I will be getting married this summer."

Everyone broke out in a congratulatory chorus as glasses clinked.

Katz' heart galloped, spurred on by happiness, pride, and affection for Darcy and Corra and their news.

And dread for what this news also meant for herself.

To Zeek, Corra's and Darcy's shared glances told him exactly how happy his cousin was with their news.

Caleb's surprise and delight were also evident.

Everyone seemed happy.

That was all he needed to know.

"Tell me about this new teaching project, Zeek," Sheila said, setting her cutlery down on her plate.

Zeek had just taken another bite of his steak, mindful of how he held his fork, feeling Katz' assessing glances.

Katz jumped in. "Miranda Brownsmith, one of the directors at the Academy, wants us to run a joint class, combining our skills."

Sheila lifted a brow.

"How is that supposed to work?" Darcy asked.

Zeek slowed his chewing, curious to hear what Katz had to say about it.

She glanced at him. At his nod, she went on. "I'm there to teach the cadets how to blend in with the upper echelons of society. And she wants Zeek to teach them street smarts. We have to show them how the skill sets are the same, despite the differences in the scenario."

"Huh," Darcy grunted, taking another sip of his drink.

"Like an addition to the role-play class," Bryah said.

"There is a certain...etiquette in both worlds." Caleb nodded.

"Right. So we have to create a curriculum and put it into practice somehow."

Darcy chuckled.

"What?" Katz asked, eyes narrowed on her brother.

He shrugged.

"Picturing Katz infiltrating street life?" Zeek asked as he brought his napkin to his lips.

Darcy nodded, eyes twinkling, as he laughed at his sister.

"How about you in a tux at a gala?" Katz shot at Zeek, her

posture stiff, eyes glittering. "Dancing," she said, extending the image.

"Is that a challenge?" Zeek leaned forward, his gorilla rising to the surface.

She tilted her head, considering him suspiciously. "A challenge to what?"

"This ought to be interesting," Caleb mumbled from behind his glass, exchanging a look with his sister, Corra.

"I bet I could blend in with your world better than you could blend in with mine."

Katz scoffed. "Of course I could. How hard can it be?"

Bryah sat wide-eyed, looking from one to the other. "Oh, Katz. You have no idea, sweetie."

Katz lost a fraction of her bravado, but she simply tossed a curl of her glossy hair over a silky shoulder, head high. "Challenge accepted." She sniffed as she reached for her drink.

Zeek wanted to reach over and crush her to him, giving her a kiss so she'd lose all her senses, too.

Her affectation of confidence, dismissive attitude, and sense of superiority made her glow. Her eyes glittered like gemstones.

He knew she'd rise to the challenge. She always did.

Katz wasn't one to back down.

He knew her better than she realized. He also knew how much she wanted him.

In the past. And now.

She just didn't know he could see through her glamor to the vulnerable kitten preening and hissing at the world, no matter how much expensive clothing and jewelry and everything else she tried to shield herself with.

She was just a kitten.

That his gorilla adored, even when she clawed and bit him.

Sometimes he enjoyed it when her kitten went to sleep. And

sometimes, he enjoyed it when she let her full-grown feline out with a growl.

What he didn't know was why she'd ghosted him.

The *real* reason.

He'd guessed it was because she realized he wasn't good enough for her—according to her parents' wishes, that was.

Despite the image she portrayed, she wasn't truly a snob. Her true value was her heart.

But at that time, his life was in shambles, lacking any real direction, riddled with addiction and a severe lack of ambition and confidence in what he could offer to the world—or her.

His family was chaos.

They were an old, established family with connections and money of their own, but their rise—especially in the last few decades—was a shady one that Zeek had been sunk into.

He glanced at his cousins.

Caleb, who'd willfully walked away.

Corra, whose mother had packed her a little bag and run away to escape their grandfather's iron-fisted control.

And no matter how many times Caleb urged Zeek to leave —the family, the fights, the Old Man's stranglehold—Zeek hadn't.

His gaze returned again and again to Katz' face.

She'd changed everything.

Made him see things a little differently. It hadn't mattered that others had told him the same thing.

She'd hit the right button.

Katz.

His Katz.

She just needed to accept that she was his.

And that he was equally hers.

He was working hard to make himself worthy of her affection.

The Academy had given him a second chance to put his

skills to good use. The fights were gone, the drugs were gone, and the sense of being out of control was gone.

Katz had inspired him to want to be better.

Now that she was back in his life, that simple fact was clearer now more than ever before.

Because Zeek was clearer now.

He saw and felt the magnetic pull between them every time her gaze slid toward him, lingering before flicking away. Some of those glances were loaded with curiosity, often with desire. After Darcy and Corra's announcement, her expression turned on him with hints of longing and sadness.

She'd left him.

And he was going to show her why she wouldn't want to leave him again.

He sipped his drink, studying her dainty movements and smiles as she talked to his family.

Their family.

He'd once heard Darcy say to Katz, "Family is everything."

He was right, with the caveat that you chose who was family and who was not.

All of them were connected now.

He looked from face to face around the table.

How at ease everyone was. His mother glowed.

I've never seen her so relaxed and happy.

If Zeek had ever had any doubts about turning against his father and grandfather, seeing his mother's expression in this moment made them all crumble.

6

The following morning, Katz reflected on the dinner at Zeek's family home.

She'd been there before. The night that had changed everything.

The last night she'd seen him until her arrival at the Academy.

It was fascinating seeing him in this environment, under these circumstances.

Previously, all of her interactions with him had been confined to whatever hotel room they had nested in.

Katz didn't see the green space around her as she walked toward the main building that housed the classes.

Cadets bustled by, intent on their own needs.

She was dimly aware of them as she recalled that first night —the very first night she'd met Zeek.

It was the night she'd arrived at The Hub to surprise Darcy with a summons from their parents to review the draft of the marriage contract they'd negotiated for him.

They'd all known it wouldn't be a smooth meeting, which

was why her parents had sent her to deliver the message. She and Darcy had always been close.

However, what she hadn't anticipated was Darcy already having a mate in Corra, who challenged the situation, which had made the next couple of weeks complicated.

Challenging, to negotiate between Darcy and their parents.

Euphoric and bittersweet, following Zeek's entrance to The Hub, minutes after she'd stirred up the chaos for her brother.

Zeek had blown into the pub on the same blustery autumn breeze she had, looking for his cousin Caleb and to meet Caleb's long-lost sister, Corra.

Apparently, it had been a busy week all around.

She vaguely remembered his reunion with them being less enthusiastic than her own with Darcy.

But, oh sweet Isis, he'd caught her attention.

The crisp air had swirled his gorilla scent around her.

Gorilla!

Of all the species to have caught her kitty's attention in *that* way…

Tall, broad shoulders, long blond hair. Everything about him screamed *bad boy*. Her eyes were immediately glued to his fantastic ass as he sauntered by her like nothing in the world could take him down.

Later, after she'd finished her well-crafted beverage, she found him leaning against The Hub's exterior wall smoking and thought, *what the hell?* She'd approached him as he took a drag off a stinking joint.

"Anything interesting to do in this— Is this even a town?"

Frowning, he'd looked down into her face then her cleavage and the rest of her. His expression softened. He offered her the joint and a wink. "Me."

The trip here had her wound into knots, and she had really wanted a release.

49

She grinned, accepted the joint, took a deep drag, pretended to consider the offer, and looked him over as he'd done to her.

Big, muscled, edgy.

The ride would be rough.

Her grin widened.

Mother would absolutely hate him.

"Rubbers?" She handed the joint back to him.

He nodded, and a spark glinted in his eye.

"Tested?"

"Negative." He rubbed the cinder off the joint, tucking the rest into a pocket.

"My room is there." She tilted her head toward the hotel behind The Hub. "End room."

He didn't look at the building but kept his attention on her face, looking at her. Looking *into* her.

Her heart tripped.

No one has ever looked at me like that.

She struggled to control her erratic pulse, maintaining her veneer of calm and collected.

Aloof.

He stepped toward her then, into her space, forcing her to look up into his face.

Her nostrils flared, taking in his scent. His gorilla, the lingering wisps of pot, the leather of his jacket... All mingled in the cool autumn breeze that encircled them in the shelter of The Hub's wall, imprinting on her mind.

This was the moment that had undone her.

Changed her forever.

She'd met him moments before. Instant attraction.

But as his large hands rose, they trailed up her arms to cradle her face.

He looked into her eyes, studied her features a long moment before he leaned in to kiss her.

She had no words for the expression in his eyes.

But he made her heart thump, her head light, and her panties wet.

His lips, warm and soft, brushed hers, and her knees buckled.

No one has ever kissed me like this.

The air was gone, but she didn't want it anyway. She just wanted the sensation of his mouth on hers to continue.

Her hands clutched at his jacket to keep herself upright.

Oh sweet Isis, I'm melting.

Finally, he released her lips, letting his hands trail back down her arms.

She sucked in a breath, which seemed to give strength to her legs again.

He'd barely touched her.

She stared at his mouth, licking her lips as her whole body throbbed.

Biting her lip, she grinned up into his self-satisfied expression.

His eyes glittered in the darkness.

She had no doubt he could smell her arousal.

"Let's go," she had said, leading him to her hotel room, where they would spend the next week.

Blinking, Katz brought her attention back to the present to ensure she didn't end up in the wrong classroom. Her heart continued to hammer with the vivid memory. Her hands shook with the power of it.

Glancing around, she spotted the washroom and ducked into it.

"Get a grip, Katz!" She stared at her flushed reflection in the mirror over the sink.

She needed to freshen up, collect herself.

You have to spend the whole day working on the curriculum for this project.

"Get your shit together," she said to herself. "You can't have him, so don't fuck this opportunity up with distractions."

No one. No one, other than Zeek, had ever made her want to run away from everything. She'd never, ever entertained the whisper of leaving her family for someone.

Her family was everything to her. Until she met him. And that terrified her.

Her purse buzzed. Extracting her phone, she frowned at the message from her mother.

I'm booked solid with meetings and contract negotiations. Meet with Sheila LeBrute to plan Darcy and Corra's official engagement party. Prepare RSVPs, compile and send me the guest list. You know what I expect and do it ASAP.

Katz sent a thumbs-up, not trusting herself to respond further without some kind of retort.

We'll discuss your contract after the party.

Gripping her phone, Katz closed her eyes, drawing steady breaths through her nose as her blood pressure soared.

As if I don't already have enough to do!

Turning the phone to Do Not Disturb, she dropped it back into her purse and withdrew her lipstick.

To calm herself, she turned her attention to touching up her makeup before completing the journey to the classroom.

To Zeek.

Hearing the click of heels, Zeek glanced up from the papers outlining the curriculum he'd drafted.

Katz.

His pulse jump-started. He sucked in a deep breath. As he released it, his pulse slowed but remained slightly elevated.

After dinner, Caleb, Corra, Darcy, and Bryah had opted to stay the night at the estate. Zeek had volunteered to drive Katz back to the campus, since they had to work in the morning anyway.

Talk had remained small. Impersonal.

In the confines of his vehicle, he heard the subtle hitches in her breathing, smelled the scents of her flip-flopping emotions, arousal and fear.

Why was she afraid?

On the outside, she maintained her composure, her voice light, edged with disinterest.

Was it because she was reminded of that night being back at the estate? The night his grandfather had ordered Zeek to hurt her? The violence and the fighting that had followed?

He'd often wondered if that was part of what had driven her away from him.

She'd witnessed firsthand what kind of damage he could do.

A thug. A brawler. Brainless muscle.

That was then.

Now, he made his own choices.

He'd given up the ring. No more fighting for profit—his grandfather's profit.

You're an instructor now, Zeek.

He rolled his shoulders, bringing his attention back to the here and now. Back to the plan, before Katz' figure moved into the open doorframe.

They had an hour before the cadets arrived for their lesson.

The idea that she feared him pushed him back into a state of discomfort.

She moved into the room.

He looked up at her then.

Her expression was cool. Guarded. Her back was straight,

though she still moved with the grace of the feline that she was. Careful and assessing. She moved toward the table, setting her bag down.

A dart of heartache dug into his chest.

I've never hurt her. Never would. Doesn't she know me better than that?

Frustration flared through him, blunting his words. "You don't need to fear me, Katz."

Her gaze flicked to his face. "I don't," she said carefully.

"Bullshit." Heat swept his body. He slapped the papers he'd been holding down on the desk beside him. "I can smell it. I smelled it last night. I smell it now."

Her complexion paled, then flushed. She looked away. "I'm not afraid of you," she insisted.

"I thought you knew me," he said, voice harsh.

Her gaze flicked back to him again. "I do. I'm not afraid of you," she growled. After a moment, she sighed, shoulders dropping. She walked over to close the classroom door.

She moved to stand before him.

He looked down into her beautiful face as she studied him.

She frowned as she looked up at him. The wall fell away to reveal her vulnerability.

She sighed, reaching for his hand.

He looked down between them. Her hands were so small supporting his much larger one.

Her fingers slid over the scars. Her touch soothed his wounded heart and made his skin tingle.

"I'm not afraid of *you*," she emphasized. "I'm afraid of myself, when I'm near you."

His lungs froze. "I don't understand."

She sighed as she stroked his hand as though she was reluctant to give him up just yet.

"I have plans. Very important plans. Obligations. Promises to fulfill. To my family and to myself."

Zeek frowned.

She went on. "I'm afraid I will derail those plans if I allow myself to become distracted by you. Because, Zeek, you're a distraction."

His whole body jerked away from her, but she held fast to his hand, anchoring him in place.

The words cut him.

A distraction.

She still wanted him. But he was just a distraction.

Good enough for a couple of weeks of intense, glorious sex.

But still her dirty little secret.

He was glad he'd never told her how he'd felt about her.

This reaffirmed he never would.

He nodded, extracting his hand from hers. "I have plans and obligations too, Katz. We have work to do."

She dropped her hands. "Colleagues. We could be friends, Zeek."

"Yup." He turned back to his printed curriculum.

At least she didn't fear him in the way he'd thought she did.

That was good, right?

The alternative didn't feel any better. He should be relieved.

He extracted a second copy of the curriculum he'd made for her and held it out. "Here's a draft we can work with."

She nodded, accepting the sheets, expression composed, wall firmly back in place.

Zeek's chest was tight as he and Caleb entered the visitor room of the prison where his father and their grandfather were incarcerated. The previous autumn, the Old Man had tried to force Corra into agreeing to his plans to strengthen his dynastic power and his control over the illegal fight rings. They'd been arrested on coercion charges, which resulted in the removal of the most powerful pillar of the underground fight world.

That morning, Caleb had called to tell him he was going in to see the Old Man.

Invitation implied, Zeek said he would drive after a moment's hesitation.

Ma. He would go. For her.

The drive was long and quiet. The relationship between Caleb and Zeek had been strained for some time, though it had eased a fraction due to Corra's influence. She'd forgiven him for his part in the Old Man's plans. Caleb hadn't. Not for that or the years before that. Not since he'd asked Zeek to leave the Old Man's grip and join the Academy with him.

Zeek hadn't. He couldn't. Not while his mother was still

living there. He wouldn't leave her alone while his father was still around.

Both men were seated at a metal table bolted to the floor, wearing bright jumpsuits and shiny handcuffs that secured them to the table.

Guards stood vigilant inside the door as Zeek and Caleb settled on the stools across from the stone-faced prisoners.

"What do you want?" the Old Man barked, looking between the two younger men.

Caleb's fist tightened on his thigh as he stared at the grizzled old dog.

Zeek spoke before Caleb could answer. "Give Mom the estate. You're not getting out of here anytime soon."

If ever.

"You mean give *you* the estate." Zeek's father, Rolland LeBrute, smirked. "After you turned on us?"

"No," Zeek said. "I don't want anything from you."

Rollo snorted.

"Why should I even consider such a brash demand?" Old Man Terry wheezed.

Zeek rolled his shoulders. "Not a demand. Request."

"And?" the Old Man prompted.

"She deserves a chance at a good life."

The Old Man barked a short laugh, exposing gums with more missing teeth than the last time Zeek had seen him. "Sheila's going to take over the fight ring?"

Caleb shook his head. "No, she's trying to run a legitimate business. But it would be much easier for her if you signed the estate over to her."

"It was all supposed to be yours, boy," the Old Man said to Caleb.

Zeek's gut tightened. The old twinge of jealousy ripped through him, but he maintained his control and dismissed it.

There was a time when it was all he'd wanted.

Things were different now.

"Mom always did as you asked." Zeek brought the conversation back to his mother.

Rollo snorted.

Except when she'd run off with Rolland LeBrute and married him against her father's wishes. A gorilla shifter, tainting the family bloodline with non-canine-shifter blood, which produced Zeek.

As a purist, the Old Man was less than pleased to learn about the union between his only daughter and a non-canine. But, as in all things, he made it work to his advantage by turning his new son-in-law gorilla shifter into his chief enforcer.

"What's in it for me?" The Old Man eyed him.

Zeek ground his teeth, staring back at the Old Man, selecting his words carefully.

Caleb answered before Zeek could. "Your legacy might actually survive, rather than crumbling into the ground or slipping into the hands of your old competitors."

That got the Old Man's attention. His eyes narrowed on Caleb. "Someone's made an offer?"

"More like someone's moving in—pressuring Aunt Sheila."

"Pressuring how?"

"Encouraging her to support their claims of dominance in the area by moving in on the fighters we're training." Zeek shrugged. "Not that she cares who's more powerful in the fight world. She just doesn't like seeing them get a raw deal."

Like the ones you forced us into.

"If that's so, then what's to say she won't just turn around and sell my property to my competitors as soon as she has control of it—*if* I were to entertain the idea?"

"Regardless of what Caleb and I think of your legacy, she does care about keeping the family name alive, especially now that Corra is getting married soon. She's going to a lot of trouble planning their official engagement party with Katz," Zeek said.

The Old Man went very still. So still Zeek wondered if he'd had a stroke.

After a long moment, the Old Man spoke. "The cats. She's marrying into that cat family."

Caleb nodded.

The Old Man's eyes jumped between Caleb and Zeek as he started to wheeze-laugh. "I'll be damned!"

Zeek's gaze slid from the Old Man to his father, who stared back with an expression of disgust.

"You never could do anything right. You may have my blood in you, but you take after your soft mother."

"You sound a little bitter about the law catching up with you, Rollo," Caleb said.

Rollo's sharp eyes darted to Caleb. "It's your fault. All of this. You turned him against us."

"You did that yourselves," Zeek said.

"*You* put us in here," Rollo growled.

"Rollo." The Old Man's voice silenced him.

Zeek saw the calculated gleam in the Old Man's eyes as he assessed his grandsons.

"If I sign everything I own over to your mother's management, I want my lawyer overseeing everything. It would only be for the duration of my incarceration, and she has to follow my direction. My competitors will never have control over what is mine. In return for my cooperation with *you*"—he turned to Caleb—"I want a reduced sentence."

"I have no control over your sentencing," Caleb said.

"The lawyer has been let go," Zeek said. "Mom will have full control over every decision."

"Until I'm released," the Old Man insisted.

Zeek and Caleb exchanged glances.

He studied his grandfather's frail form. Prison had aged him further than his already ancient years. His skin hung now on a bowed frame, where it hadn't before. His hair and skin were thinner.

"Power of attorney and sole inheritor," Zeek pushed.

Rollo stiffened, scowling at his progeny, and then he laughed. To Caleb he said, "You're okay with him taking everything for himself when his mother dies?"

Caleb smiled. "I don't give a shit about any of it."

Zeek spoke to the Old Man. "You know Mom will share it out equally."

He nodded. "There isn't a crooked bone in that woman's body. It's why she never really fit in with my work." He sucked in a breath and blew it out, hands flat on the table. "Still. I won't have my rivals touching one cent of my money or blade of grass of my estate. I want them eradicated," he said, turning his full attention to Caleb.

Caleb blinked. "Tell me everything you know and the Furry United Coalition can move in."

The Old Man snorted. "I ain't no rat, boy. You wanted to be a fancy agent then be a fancy agent. I won't do your job for you." He lifted his gaze to the guards by the door and raised his voice as he got to his feet. "We're about done here."

"You'll sign over to Mom?" Zeek said as he and Caleb rose from their seats and moved aside when the guards came forward.

"Secure my property from my rivals. Then we'll talk." He held his wrists up so the guard could unfasten them from the table.

Zeek and Caleb watched the older men as they were led out of a door on the far side of the room. Rollo smirked at Zeek over his shoulder.

Zeek's gut tightened.

Caleb's hand clapped Zeek's shoulder. "We knew he

wouldn't just agree. There's always a catch. It was just a matter of finding what exactly he wanted."

"He wants out, and for some reason, he thinks we can do something about it."

They made their way out of the prison to Zeek's truck.

"Do you think Rollo will inform for us?" Caleb asked, settling into the front seat.

"He'd need a good reason to. Everyone has guys in and out of prison. Snitching isn't good for anyone's health. He definitely won't do it while the Old Man is alive. Not while there's the slightest chance he can still get something out of his long years of loyalty."

"Loyalty." Caleb snorted.

"As *he* sees it, yes." Zeek shrugged. "But he knows more about everyone than the Old Man does." Rollo believed his loyalty would lead to his taking over control of the family when the Old Man kicked it, especially after Caleb ran away to the FUCNA after his father died.

"And he'd want the same deal."

"Yup," Zeek said, throwing the truck into gear before pulling out of the lot.

"FUC would never agree to letting either of them out early."

"Then I guess you're on your own, man."

Zeek felt Caleb's gaze drilling into him as he drove.

"Am I?"

"No," he said before the thoughts could fully form. His gut knew what Caleb's brain was working up to. "Absolutely not."

Caleb's voice was soft when he spoke again. "It's a good way for you to redeem yourself."

Zeek's hands tightened on the steering wheel so hard it groaned.

"Isn't that what you're trying to do? Redeem yourself? Handling things, helping your mom, teaching at the Academy. You've done a total one-eighty."

61

Zeek's voice was as tight as his fists. "I swore I'd never go back into a ring. Never go back to that world."

"You're renowned in the fight scene, Zeek. While you're dazzling everyone in the ring, as your manager on the sidelines, I can find what I need to close this case. *We* can close this case together. It would be for a good cause."

"You want me to break the first promise I made to myself?"

Caleb rubbed his hands over his face, but with a glance, Zeek saw the determined set of his cousin's jaw.

For him, FUC came first.

Zeek felt as though he'd been sucker-punched right before the words formed in his thoughts and he spit them out.

"You planned this. You knew what he'd say, and that would give you leverage to pressure me into doing this."

Caleb didn't answer.

"If I go back into that ring, I might not be able to leave it again. You and Darcy should be able to handle this. You're trained for it."

"If we do our jobs right, there won't be any illegal rings left. At least not in this district. And we both know I can only do this with your help."

"You're going to have to do it without me. I'm not that guy anymore."

"Staff, how'd it go with Old Man Terry?" Darcy Karak addressed Caleb Terry by his nickname as they met in the Academy parking lot. He was still getting used to using his friend and partner's given name now that they weren't cadets anymore.

He'd been waiting for him to return after his meeting at the prison.

"Exactly how I thought it would."

"Zeek pissed?"

He'd watched Caleb and Zeek exit the truck. Zeek headed toward campus without a further word to Caleb.

"Yep."

"Shame. I didn't think he'd resist helping you out. Especially given the circumstances of how things went down."

"That's why he doesn't want anything to do with our case. Clean break."

"No such thing," Darcy said.

"I know that. And deep down he does too. I'll get him to come around."

"And if he doesn't?"

Caleb shrugged. "He'll have to. Have you talked to Katz yet?"

Darcy dropped his gaze.

"I know you don't want to drag Katz into this investigation any more than I wanted to pull Zeek into it."

"She has zero training."

"She has valuable knowledge."

"She's also swamped planning the engagement party with your aunt. Along with her work at the Academy, I doubt she can find the time to help us with some reconnaissance."

"After the party?"

Darcy sighed.

His parents would be seriously unhappy if he jeopardized their family image. And he was considering doing just that by even thinking about getting Katz involved in this case.

But she knew *everyone* who was anyone, just like their mother did.

And if it was as he and Caleb suspected—that wealthy bene-factors were investing in the illegal rings—then they needed someone who could identify them. And then they could follow the money.

Darcy knew a lot of the wealthy families in the shifter

community. But he had nowhere near the knowledge that Katz did after a lifetime of shadowing their mother during her networking events.

He blew out another breath. "I'll talk to her."

Caleb clapped him on the shoulder.

"Don't wrinkle my suit, man." Darcy glared at his partner, who just released him with a grin. "Come on. We have work to do in the city. I have a lead there's going to be an event soon."

They got into Darcy's car.

It started with a roar and settled into a rumble. He cast Caleb another glance.

"What?" Caleb demanded.

"I also heard there may be fighters that were experimented on."

"Fuck," Caleb swore, rubbing a hand through his hair. "Fuck!" He slammed a hand on the dash.

"It was only a matter of time before someone decided to cash in on the novelty."

Darcy knew Caleb was thinking about Bryah, who had, in fact, survived one of the many experimental facilities FUC had shut down across the continent and around the world.

The more novel a fighter, the bigger the draw and the more money could be made.

With some of the organizers and benefactors, it didn't matter if the fighters were willing or not. They would have their event, and they would make their money.

That was why they were working so hard to shut them down, but to stop the forced fighting, they needed evidence.

Darcy navigated to the car toward the nearest highway headed southwest. "Don't worry. She's safe at the Academy."

Caleb huffed a laugh. "As long as I don't tell her anything about what we're doing, it will stay that way."

Bryah had a knack for getting herself into trouble. The worst of it.

"We just have to figure out how to handle this carefully so that we get what we need and no one is at risk," Darcy said.

"Right." Caleb blew out a breath. "I'll talk to Bear at The Hub and Old Carl at the hotel and ask them to let me know if they hear anything."

"I talked to Joe Suricatta while you were with Zeek. He'll set up some alerts and have them forwarded to us. Miranda and Chase are aware of what we're doing in the area and why. They'll provide backup if we need it, but we should try to handle it on our own if we can."

Caleb nodded. "This is our first big case. Can't screw it up."

"We won't. I know how important this is to you," Darcy said, glancing at his partner and friend. "We got this."

8

A week later, Katz was sick of studying seating diagrams, guest lists, card stocks, and fonts but especially the guest list. Culling and re-adding, over and over. She struggled to control her temper so she didn't hiss at any of the students.

She closed her eyes and drew a deep breath. Held it. Calmed herself. And on the release, Katz resolved to separate her obligations to her family from what she was doing at the Academy. She opened her eyes and smiled.

"Please refer to the PDF download in your online syllabus, section 1-2: Dinner."

The large screen at the front of the room displayed an image of an impossibly complex display of a banquet place setting.

"There is a diagram of this image in the syllabus, along with labels and diagrams of seating positions with corresponding placing titles. Look over it every day and you'll absorb it eventually."

Between curriculum planning and revisions and party planning and revisions, she was tired and testy.

Communication from her mother was abrupt and demanding.

At least working with Sheila was a balm to her nerves. Sweet and calm. Cooperative.

The extra work also afforded her excuses to limit her time with Zeek.

She strode to the other side of the screen as she clicked the remote to advance the slide. "Don't worry about the length of the table if it's like this one." She gestured toward the image of a long banquet table. "In a setting like this, you would focus on small blocks of space. Your companions directly beside you. Your facing partner and their adjacent neighbors. Groups of six, including yourself."

Zeek stood motionless in the corner of the room, observing her lecture along with everyone else.

She'd noted that he'd had some familiarity with table etiquette during his mother's dinner the previous week.

Before then, she assumed he'd be completely uninitiated in this type of environment.

She was wrong.

Still, she noted the intensity with which he observed her presentation.

"The pinwheel settings of a circular table are very different. Here your circle can be as much as eight, ten, or twelve depending on how intimate the organizer wishes the experience to be. Regardless of how large the table is, reduce your focus to your immediate neighbors, but always be open and acknowledging of those beyond that fuzzy area.

"Always be aware of who surrounds you—from the moment you enter the venue. Ideally, you would find out who the other guests are before you've chosen your shoes for the night."

Katz gave further instruction on the settings, the functions of the placement, and how to properly use a napkin and hold a glass.

Zeek remained quiet, following along like everyone else.

Her nerves were bundled under his scrutiny.

She'd already underestimated him. Maybe he knew even more than she did?

She doubted that, but still, how much did she really know about the man she'd had blissful nights with all those months ago?

Sure they'd talked. But about other things.

Like dreams, incredibly detailed and vague at the same time.

I want to sail around the world.

But not why.

I want to negotiate the toughest contracts.

But not with whom.

I'd like to xyz...

But neither ever said "with you" or what it meant.

Just fragile facts. A veneer of future hopes.

Many times, as she lay in Zeek's arms, her fingertip lazily tracing the ridges of his muscles, she'd wanted to propose that they run away and do these wild things—just the two of them.

Build something of their own together.

She didn't.

She had obligations to her family.

And he was Zeek, by his own words his grandfather's thug. He'd laugh about his lack of ambition only minutes after murmuring about how he'd do something different from how his father did it.

She often felt that way about how her mother ran things. But Mother wouldn't alter her methodology.

Katz stared at the diagram.

Her mother even had her own dinner party methods.

Katz' eyes flicked from the display to Zeek and back.

What was she thinking? Who was she kidding?

Katz, this is the most ridiculous thing you've ever done—thinking

she'd take you seriously by becoming an instructor at the most presti-
gious Academy for shifters. Teaching table etiquette and dress and
accessory language? No wonder Mother doesn't trust you enough to
hand over the family business.

She's testing you with this party for Darcy. A jab at what you're
doing here.

She'll never retire peacefully.

I take after Daddy too much. A caracal. I will never be the lioness
that Mother is.

Her vision blurred, and she blinked.

"Ms. Karak?" Zeek's low voice drew her attention to his concerned expression.

She smiled. "Shall we move to the other room for the practical portion of the lesson?"

He nodded and opened the door.

They'd set up the unused classroom next to theirs with two full-length banquet tables, complete with tablecloths, cards indicating each setting, and even dressed chairs.

The cadets followed their instructors, and Katz motioned them toward the table and stood back to watch what they did.

Some moved the same as they always did.

A male student dragged a chair back from the table and flopped down, not paying attention to the details.

Corra tapped him on the shoulder, pointing at the crisp white card with her name printed in bold calligraphy. He squinted at it, then rose from the chair in search of his own little card. He grinned when he found his name waiting on the next table over, three chairs from the end.

Other students added extra flourishes to their movements. A couple of the male cadets suavely gestured toward their female colleagues to sit as they held their chairs for them.

Now they were starting to get into character, although overdoing it a little bit.

Katz smiled, surveying the rest of the room.

A few more looked like they were trapped in a nightmare, keeping their distance.

"Bryah?" Katz drew her attention, noting how her hands were curled into her chest.

Wide-eyed, Bryah's gaze flew to Katz. "I don't want to break anything. It all looks so pretty and perfect."

"Oh, sweetie, you'll be fine. Just settle in." Katz encouraged her.

Bryah carefully extracted her chair and gingerly sat on it without moving it any closer to the table. Hands gripping her knees, she peered over the place setting, studying the array of tableware.

While Bryah was hyper-focused on remaining as far from the breakables as possible, another student, the same one that had moved on from Corra's chair, was sprawled and flipping a steak knife end over end, catching it by the handle like it was a bread stick.

Others had already broken out into role play and were talking like nineteenth-century aristocrats, pinkies in the air and all.

She sighed. The cadets had somehow devolved into a room full of seventh graders in a matter of minutes.

How to put this into a teaching moment.

"You." She pointed at the knife-flipper.

He caught the piece of cutlery mid-flip between thumb and forefinger. Eyebrow raised over a challenging grin, he waited for her admonishment.

"Bold, over the top, with a blatant disregard for strict conventions. Slap a tux on you, ditch the knife, and you'll be the stickiest honey trap of the party."

His complexion darkened four shades as he swallowed his embarrassment and gingerly placed the knife back where it belonged.

All chair scraping, dish clattering, and chatter stopped as

everyone looked wide-eyed between the knife-flipper and Katz.

Zeek chuckled.

"Whereas Bryah, here"—Katz walked over to Bryah's chair —"would also draw attention to herself by the power of her discomfort. Neither—what's your name?"

"Vo."

"Neither Bryah nor Vo blend in—yet—but they can still make the situation work for them in their own unique ways. Whether you ooze rebellious non-conformist or quirky and endearing, you can still make it work, so long as you know the basic rules. Know the rules before you decide which ones to flaunt or break in order to achieve a specific desired outcome. This is valuable knowledge whether you're infiltrating solo or with a team. These two would shine, giving the rest of the team time to go grey and get needed information from different vantage points."

Everyone settled into their places properly, prepared to listen.

"Good, let's begin. You'll learn faster if you help each other." She stood at the head of one of the tables. "Which utensils do you start with and why?"

The cadets began conferring among themselves to determine the answer.

Katz glanced toward Zeek, who still stood off to the side, observing.

He smiled and nodded in her direction.

She relaxed a little.

Miranda Brownsmith wouldn't have given Katz an instructing position and paired her with Zeek for a special project if she didn't think the skills Katz offered wouldn't be useful to FUC agents.

Zeek spotted Katz as she entered the next classroom, which they'd set up as a sort of club atmosphere.

She approached where he stood at the front of the room as the cadets moved in, drifting toward chairs and tables set in clusters and in a line along one wall to simulate a bar.

"Stickiest honey trap of the party, huh?" he whispered as she passed him. "Firsthand experience?"

Her eyes flashed, and her delicate skin turned pink as she smiled. "Wouldn't you like to know?"

He did. But he would never say so. Instead, voice low so only she could hear, he said, "I thought you were a honey trap at one point."

She turned and regarded him, brow raised. "Funny. There were times I wondered that of you too."

His brow rose to match hers, and a slow grin spread across his face. "I had no idea you were so suspicious, kitten."

She stiffened. "Nor I of you, monkey," she spat. "Don't call me kitten." She hissed.

He chuckled. "No need to hiss, at least not right now. We have work to do." He nodded toward the cadets, eying them curiously.

She straightened, tossed a long curl over her shoulder, planted a smile on her face, and spun around to face them.

"Now that everyone is settled, it's instructor LeBrute's turn to show us how to turn our strengths into muscles... ehm...weapons."

A few students chuckled. Bryah and Corra grinned at Katz.

Zeek cleared his throat and stepped forward, drawing their attention.

"Although the tone of this setting is very different, the approach that Ms. Karak showed you in the other room isn't. It's all about image. Power—yes, but a different kind. Control. Also, like Ms. Karak instructed, there will be those that can go grey and blend in unnoticed. Those who know this world intimately. Those that don't will always unintentionally draw attention. Use it."

His gaze traveled over the faces, most of whom he knew from his martial arts class.

"This is where we learn when to show our physical power and when not to. And just because we don't have the rules of a hierarchical table arrangement doesn't mean there aren't any. They just come in different packaging."

"Like hot gorilla instructors," someone stage-whispered.

Some of the female students giggled, and a few males rolled their eyes. Nearly everyone grinned, including Katz.

"Sounds like you have a fan," she said.

"Have you seen this guy in action?" one female said. "He's amazing in the gym."

"Forget the gym. Have you seen him in the ring?" a male said.

Zeek froze. His gut snapped tight.

Katz' gaze turned curious as she looked at him.

"What ring?" the female said. "You mean like a fight, right?"

"Oh my god, that's so awesome. You're an actual ring fighter?" someone squeaked.

"Was. Not anymore," Zeek growled.

Katz' continued study must have noted his discomfort at the turn of subject. She glanced at her watch. "Time is running short. We still have much material to cover today."

They completed the lesson, having successfully covered all of the scheduled material for that day.

The last of the cadets were filing out of the classroom door when Katz approached Zeek as she slung her large purse over her shoulder. "That went well."

"Better than hoped." He stuffed the last of his printouts into his leather bag and zipped it closed. "Now to do it all again tomorrow."

She sighed, shoulders drooping. "This is more work than I

thought it would be. Especially with the party planning I have to do with your mother."

He chuckled. "And you've been here, what? A week? Two?"

She pulled a face.

"It gets easier after the first couple of weeks and the kinks are worked out."

"Kinks," she echoed, skin flushing again.

"Hiccups, kitten. I wasn't referring to anything other than innocent kinks, but if you want to explore non-innocent versions of kink, I'd be happy to oblige you."

She gaped.

He laughed at her discomfort, but he knew she was visualizing. "We can work on our…strengths tonight at my place. You know, work those muscles."

She licked her lips. Her eyes swept his chest and arms.

Did she even know when she did it? Was it a tell or a signal?

Either way, she was interested.

She caught herself. "Not interested. Colleagues, co-workers only," she reminded him with a stern look.

"Right."

He wondered how long it would actually take him to get her naked if he put a little effort into it. He'd been thinking about it a lot lately. All week, in fact. Since she'd called him a distraction, which ruffled his fur. And being near her every day and pretending like he didn't want to scoop her up and climb the nearest building to roar from the top with his prize… Well, that didn't help.

Her gaze remained stern as she stared at him.

"Yes, ma'am."

She scowled at him, turned toward the door, and practically stomped out of the room.

He followed her out, closed and locked the door. He turned to find her still waiting partway down the hall.

He lifted a brow as he approached.

"Dinner."

"Sorry?"

"Dinner. You said you cook. Prove it."

"Well, yes I did, but..." He noted the uplifted challenge in her tilted chin. "Okay."

A game then?

She was going to prove to him how determined she was to pursue her goal of proving her independence to her mother, no matter how much she wanted him. She wasn't going to let him wear her down.

Zeek's gorilla wanted to thump his chest and take up the challenge. To him, the chase was on.

They walked along the halls to the first junction, where they would go their separate ways.

But he took a moment to reel it back. There was no reason one of them had to lose. He could show her they could both succeed and have a little fun doing it.

"Steak?"

"Of course."

He glanced at his watch. He'd have to make a quick trip into town to grab fresh meat from the butcher shop after his last class.

"Seven."

She nodded.

He grinned. Let the wooing begin.

FAR, FAR AWAY IN LAS VEGAS...

He almost had the bastard. Almost...almost...and lost him.

Trent Aslan glanced up as Jerry came in through the door.

"Mail," Jerry said, dropping a stack of envelopes on the coffee table of Trent's Bellagio suite.

Trent sighed, pushing it aside with the heel of his foot as he continued to work the controller of his video game. "Later."

The target came back into his line of sight, and he went in pursuit.

Pop!

"Dub!" He threw his hands in the air. "Third of the day."

"That's great," Jerry said, walking in front of the screen while Trent's avatar was in the lounge before another round. "One of those envelopes is fancy stock. You should open it. It's been forwarded."

Trent shrugged. "Told you. Not interested."

"The casinos won't extend our credit anymore. Can you float us?"

"Nope. My allowance is maxed. Move. My game is starting."

"Open the mail first and I'll move."

"Dammit, Jerry, I'm on a roll. Don't kill my streak."

Jerry turned and glanced at the screen. "You've got twenty-three seconds, bro."

"Fine." Trent stomped his feet on the floor and snatched at the stack of mail, pulling the crisp envelope free from the bills and junk. With another quick glance at the screen, he ripped it open and pulled the card out.

"Invitation," he grunted, tossing it back onto the table and snatching up his controller. "Six seconds. Move."

Jerry plucked the card from the table and dropped down onto the couch next to Trent, jostling him in the process.

"Dude, I'm trying to scope the grounds here."

"You are cordially invited to the official engagement party of Mr. Darcy Karak and Ms. Corra Terry. Karak. Why is that familiar?"

"My fiancée is a Karak. Damn, got tanked. Quit distracting me," Trent growled.

"Fiancée, huh?" Jerry rubbed a thumb over the card stock

then slapped it against his opposing palm. "So, this Darcy is a future brother-in-law?"

Trent nodded, focused on his aim. He pulled the trigger, and the enemy dropped. "I'm engaged to the youngest daughter, Katharine. Darcy is one year older than her. Once he's married, we're next."

"So, you're getting married soon."

Trent shrugged. "Yup." His lips popped on the "p."

"She's loaded?"

"Uhnhuh."

Damn! I'm dying here.

He sucked in a breath and ducked around a barrel as the screen flashed red. "Don't worry about Katz. She's cool. You'll like her. Nothing like her mother."

"Mother? Will she be a problem for us?"

"Dunno. Why would she be?"

"Never mind. Just don't want anyone to mess with our friendship, y'know."

Trent glanced up at Jerry's change of tone. "Don't worry, man. You, me, and Woods, we're tight. Bros for life. Where is Woodrow anyway?"

"Still in Candy's room. He'll be down before breakfast buffet ends." He patted his stomach.

"I thought he was with Lily. Man, that guy taps everything he sees."

"Lily was last week. He's a woodpecker. What do you expect?" Jerry said. "You should book us plane tickets for this engagement party this afternoon."

"Don't really want to go."

Jerry paced the room.

"We should go and see what this new family of yours is like."

"Don't need to. I know them." Trent's thumbs slammed the controller.

"Hmm, the RSVP address is British Columbia, Canada. I've heard there's a solid fight ring in that area. Shifter fighters, I mean."

Trent's attention was immediately diverted. "Fight ring?"

Jerry nodded. "In fact, it's supposed to be one of the best north of the border. Very lucrative."

Trent licked his lips. "It has been a while since I could bet on something interesting."

"Sure has. This place is getting stale, right?"

Trent nodded, picturing the excitement of betting on live fights. "Illegal fights?"

"Very."

"Shifters? What kinds? Anyone we might know?"

Jerry shrugged. "We should go and see for ourselves."

"I don't think Katz would be into that sort of thing. Her mother most certainly wouldn't be."

"They don't have to know our business. Besides, it's not like they'd ever know, right? They've probably never even heard of underground fighting."

Trent frowned. "I don't know, Jerry. Mrs. Karak has always seemed to know everything about everybody."

Jerry laughed. "Sounds like you're afraid of her."

"You're not wrong." Trent chuffed a short laugh. "I've known the Karaks most of my life, and she's…intense. Like she can see right into your brain."

Jerry waved the card in the air. "Looks to me like she'll be distracted with engagement stuff anyway."

"Think Woods will want to go? He seems to be having a good time here hanging out with the dancers."

Jerry grinned. "I think Woodrow will want to check out the girl fighters."

Trent gave a decisive nod. "Okay, I just need another dub. Then I'll make the calls."

Jerry glanced at his watch with a frown then grabbed a controller. "We can team up for your win. It'll go faster."

Trent's tummy tightened, and his heart fluttered. "We make an awesome team. We'll get a bunch of dubs." He was almost giddy with the promise of the wins.

9

Why, oh why am I so damned impulsive?

Katz grumbled as she continued to admonish herself for giving in to her baser instincts.

I miss him—talking to him.

The memory of his kisses barreled through her head. She shuttered them away and focused on the food.

And she never could resist the promise of a good steak.

How will he prepare it?

Au jus? Gravy? Charred and crisp with an oozy middle?

"Bet it turns out like shoe leather," she grumbled to curb the saliva gathering in her mouth. She held up two dinner dresses, trying to decide which he'd like more.

Then she checked herself.

Katz, what the sweet Isis are you doing? You don't want to end up in bed with him.

Like hellcat we don't. Her kitty responded with a little *merow*.

"Stop that," she hissed at her reflection.

But we should see if his stamina is as long-lived as it was when we had our marathons of gorilla-kitty love sessions.

"No, we shouldn't," she said aloud.

Or if he's still strong enough to support us when we—

"Stop it!" she shouted, trying to dispel the memories of acrobatic sex with Zeek before the reel really got going.

She threw both dresses onto the bed and stomped back into her closet.

A knock at the door drew her out, with more outfits clutched in her hands. She tossed them on the nearby chair and went to the front door and ripped it open. "Yes?"

A small man stood on the small porch, peering at her. It was her neighbor Floyd. "Oh, hello again. I have very sensitive hearing, and thought I heard an argument happening and wanted to ensure you were all right?" He blinked up at her.

She blinked back.

He heard that?

She'd have to remember that if she…. No. She ended that thought right there. She wasn't going to have sex with Zeek. Or anyone else. So it didn't matter how sensitive her neighbor's hearing was because there wouldn't be anything to overhear.

Other than her arguing with herself, apparently.

She realized she hadn't answered. "Uhm, yes, I'm fine. Like I said last time, just practicing some lines—material for a class I'm teaching."

"Well, okay. But if you need anything—even just someone to talk to. I'm a good listener and I'm just next door. " He waved toward a house to her left.

Away from the direction of Zeek's house, she noted.

Good, her kitty thought. Vocal expression is critical during lovemaking for a cat.

No. No. No!

"Thank you. I'll keep that in mind," she said after another drawn-out moment and quickly shut the door.

Shower.

Change.

Sedative?

It's just dinner. Calm yourself.
Remember: Aloof.

The doorbell alerted Zeek that his guest had arrived.

He glanced at the clock.

Katz.

He turned the burner down on the stove, lowered the volume of his Bluetooth speaker, and strode toward the front door.

Opening it with a flourish, he froze. His gaze slid down Katz' person from the perfect crown of her glossy hair down to the fresh touches of makeup, along her immaculate red dress outlining her curves and down her silky bare legs to her shiny stiletto pumps.

He swallowed. Then swallowed again.

His voice barely above a whisper he said, "Perfection."

"Do you have wine?" She brushed past him in the open door, leaving a subtle trail of peony perfume.

He drew a breath so deep he was sure peony fields would sprout in his lungs then closed the front door.

His gorilla floated after her on a cloud of her perfume.

She moved through the living room, inspecting the little things on the shelves and walls and the random bowls of fruit Zeek had in every room.

"You've made it yours," she said, selecting an orange from the nearest fruit bowl to study.

"I spend most of my time here, now."

He was more at home here than he'd ever been anywhere else, including his grandfather's estate. *Especially* his grandfather's estate.

I've never belonged there.

Maybe that was why he was avoiding his mother's push for

him to take over the family business and move it into legitimacy. No, it was more than that.

"Hungry? Everything is ready. I just need to throw the steaks on the heat."

"I am." She smiled, replacing the orange in its bowl of citrus fruits.

"Rare?"

"Medium rare. Wine?" she asked again.

"On the table, next to the berries."

"I'll open it. You cook."

In no time, he had the steaks plated and garnished. One last check to ensure the stove and vent were turned off, and he carried the plates to the table. Katz was back in the living room, perusing his bookshelf.

"I didn't know you were a reader," she said when she noticed his presence.

He shrugged. "The hotels we locked ourselves in didn't exactly have libraries."

She smiled. "Even if they had, I don't think either of us would have noticed. I certainly wouldn't have at any rate."

He lifted a brow. Letting the comment slide by, he reached for her hand and said, "Dinner is ready, Ms. Karak." He dipped his head to brush his lips over her satiny fingers.

Goose flesh rose on her arm at the contact. She extracted her hand but allowed her fingers to linger within his as she did so.

She settled at his table and poured the wine while he served the accompanying potatoes and salad.

"Smells amazing."

"As do you."

She lifted her eyes to his in a coy manner then turned her focus back to her plate. His attention was glued to her movements as she cut into the steak, speared the piece with her fork, and brought it to her plump lips.

Breath held, he waited, heart pounding.

Eyes closed, she chewed, expression blissful as she moaned. "Mmm…"

He was already aroused by her presence. At the sound of her low moan, he hardened then hardened more as memories of her moans during their shared ecstasy flooded his brain. Becoming lightheaded, he sought an anchor. Reaching for the glass of wine he held it over the table.

Seeing this, Katz swallowed her mouthful of food and reached for her own glass.

"To old memories and new partnerships," Zeek said.

She repeated his words with a smile and touched the glass to his with a soft clink.

His gaze lingered on her lips, recalling her unique taste as he sipped the wine. Nothing could compare.

He cut into his steak, watching her hands over her plate as he did so, recalling the feel of her fingers on his skin, exploring, stroking, gripping.

He barely tasted the seasoned meat as his attention turned to the low neckline of her red dress and her generous breasts. His mouth watered, not for the meal on the plate but for the feast seated across from him.

He wanted to run his fingers through her silky hair.

She sipped from her wine again, a measured sip. Her tongue skimmed her lip to collect an errant drop.

He also recalled the sensation of her tongue tracing the ridges and valleys of his abdomen… and lower.

He cleared his throat. "Tell me what you have been doing in these last months since… since the night my father and grandfather were arrested for coercion."

"Working. Just working in my family's business. Maintaining and strengthening my mother's legacy."

"Do you enjoy it?"

She dipped her head. "I do, actually. Most of the time. I

just..." She sighed. "I just want the illusion that I have a choice now and then."

"I know what you mean. It was like that working for my grandfather. He wanted something done. I did it. No questions."

"Yes, exactly! Like jump in the exact way before they think of how high. It's exhausting."

They both sipped more wine.

"Have you figured out what you want?"

"Not quite." She shrugged. "I know what I don't want."

"Which is?"

"The sensation of being smothered. The claustrophobic feeling of having every waking second dictated to me."

"Sovereignty."

She blinked. "Yes. I mean I do want to work for the family. I love seeing my parents and siblings every day and knowing we're maintaining the legacy Mother built for us and our descendants—if we don't screw it all up once she's gone." She cut another piece of steak.

"You won't."

Her gaze lifted to his face. "How can you be so sure?"

"You're intelligent. You're driven. You're amazing." He smiled. "I remember how determined you were to work things out for Darcy. How bold you were, taking the initiative to negotiate with my grandfather. If he hadn't been such a megalomaniac, I'm sure you'd have succeeded." His gaze studied her face a few seconds. "You did succeed where your mother was concerned, right? She eased off, and he and Corra are exploring life together in relative peace. Relative, because being a FUC agent... there's little peace involved."

Katz was quiet a long while, having turned her attention back to her plate. After several more mouthfuls of food, she swallowed and said, "I'm next."

"Next for what?" A black pit gaped with a thunderous crack in his gut. His instinct knew the answer before his brain did.

"Marriage contract negotiations."

Zeek put his fork down and stared at her. Her face remained tilted down. When she reached for her glass, her gaze slid to the far side of the room over his shoulder.

"You can negotiate yourself out of it."

She flinched.

"Unless you don't want to? You want this contract? This marriage? Do you know the guy?"

She nodded. "I've known him all my life."

The remainder of Zeek's light mood fizzled out of him as he slumped on his chair. Another mouthful of potatoes, which suddenly tasted like paste. He reached for the wine glass to wash it down, but it tasted sour.

"Do you want this contract?" he asked again.

"It doesn't matter."

"It does." His hand reached toward hers on the table, but he pulled back before touching her.

"No, it doesn't. I agreed to it. As part of the negotiations for Darcy's freedom to choose his own partner, I agreed to honor the contract my parents had for me and Trent Aslan. No matter what."

"Aslan." Zeek frowned. He knew that name but couldn't recall from where. He looked up, meeting her eyes.

She stared at him, her expression defiant despite the tears in her eyes.

"Hey," he said softly, rising from his seat. An instant later he was next to her, pulling her to her feet, his arms around her. "It's not going to happen. I won't let it."

She sighed into his chest, her body melting against his. "It's practically done, Zeek. I can't go back on my agreement."

"Talk to Darcy. Get him to help you."

"No," she snapped, pulling away from Zeek. "He can't know. Ever. It would rip him if he knew."

"Okay," he soothed, pulling her to him again. Jesus, it felt good to hold her in his arms again.

She belongs right here. With me. Always.

His mind whirled with ways to break a contract. He had no experience with contracts in the paper and ink way of doing things. He'd always been sent to negotiate in a "with his fists" kind of way.

It wasn't like he could go and beat up Katz' parents to comply with her wishes.

Maybe he could go and beat up this guy, Trent. Scare him out of the agreement.

What would that do to the family, though? He recalled the purpose of the unions were to strengthen the family and the business in some way.

I don't care.

"I'm not going to let them force you into a marriage you don't want."

She looked up into his face. Her smile was sad, but gentle, her face flushed from the wine.

"That's what I've always loved about you, Zeek. You're so, so sweet."

Loved about me?

He couldn't resist.

He bent, touching his lips to hers.

His gorilla sighed.

Opening his eyes, he kissed her forehead.

Her eyes remained closed, a frown marred the usually smooth line of her brow.

When she looked up into his face, she studied him with shimmering gold-green eyes.

"Zeek," she whispered. Further words stuck in her throat.

She swallowed and tried again. "We both know I desire you. I want you. I want to be with you."

His heart soared.

"But not at the expense of my goals. I've worked too hard to allow your soulful eyes, glorious hair, and really, really gorgeous body to distract me."

Ouch.

It didn't matter that she probably hadn't intended to shred his heart.

His spine straightened as he considered her.

Her words were in complete opposition to her body language.

Usually when he caught her staring at him, she looked as though she were ready to pounce and devour. Which was cool.

Until she suddenly turned on her aloof mode and lashed out with needle-sharp claws.

She was starting to leave little scars in her wake.

Zeek was getting tired of it.

Her full lips tightened, which was a tell that there was more she wasn't saying.

"Soulful eyes? Glorious hair and gorgeous body, huh?" He smirked. "Distraction?"

She nodded, lips tightening further.

A devious impulse took him over.

Fuck it.

"What kind of distraction? This kind of distraction? Something like this?" he demanded as his fingers flicked down the front of his shirt, releasing buttons down to his navel before she had time to blink.

Instead, her eyes widened, fixed on the little glimpses of his abs the fabric allowed as he moved.

She opened her mouth to speak, but no words emerged. Instead, her tongue slid out to moisten her lips as her gaze flicked back and forth between his belly button and his eyes, with little appreciative sweeps of his chest in between, as though a laser pointer darted all over his torso.

He chuckled, rolling his shoulders to shrug out of the shirt, ensuring every muscle flexed in tandem.

She bit her lip, trying to stifle a moan as she breathed his name.

Yeah, I'm an asshole.

But her self-absorbed jerking of the leash she'd wrapped around his throat was pretty asshole-ish too.

"I have goals too, Katharine. Maybe I don't want *you* distracting me from *my* future." His voice was harsher than he'd meant it to be. "Maybe I have important obligations, too, which don't involve wasting time on you."

She stepped back, stung.

"Or maybe you're more important to me than any of it." He shrugged. "Which is it?"

Her brows rose. She looked confused, insulted and incredibly curious. "What? What the—what? What are you saying?"

He tapped the end of her nose with his fingertip. "Wouldn't you like to know."

She batted his hand away from her face, but he'd already turned away from her, chucking his wadded shirt onto a nearby chair.

I can pose and be alluring and confuse the hell out of her too.

He released the elastic holding his long blond hair back from his face, shaking out his mane.

He turned, sloping his body with a slight twist into the perfect ab-display pose, hips forward, shoulders back, hair brushing his shoulders.

He drew a hand across his lower abdomen, drawing her attention. Teasing.

She scowled at his hand. Her small hands balled into little fists.

"I'm sorry. Am I distracting you from something important?" He lifted his brows, exhibiting his most innocent expression. "Hmm. I'm tired. I think I'll turn in now." He glanced at his watch. It wasn't even eight o'clock. "Long day," he murmured, unbuckling his belt.

He peeked at her from under his brows.

She gaped at him, cheeks flushed a deep bronzy peach.

Belt gaping, he reached for the top button and fly before he looked up at her. "Oh, are you still here? I thought you had important things to do. Don't let me distract you."

Her beautiful, beautiful skin turned scarlet all the way down to her cleavage, spreading across her chest toward the neckline of her red dress.

His jeans hit the floor.

His boxers rode low on his trim hips, full erection belying the aloof, dismissive attitude he threw at her.

The air crackled through the living room, drawing the heady scent of her arousal toward him.

"See you in the classroom, Ms. Karak," he growled then turned his back on her and strode toward his bedroom, closing the door with a definitive click.

His balls ached as he listened hard over the pounding of his chest.

After a full minute, her heels thumped across the carpet and then snapped on the tile as she made her way to the front door.

The door thundered shut behind her.

He drew a deep breath.

Tomorrow is going to be hell.

Somewhere around town...

Trent, Jerry, and Woodrow pulled their rental around the corner of a pub called The Hub and into the parking lot of the hotel they'd booked a room at.

They had rooms waiting for him at the Terry estate where the party was going to be, but he and his buddies had arrived in the area a few days early, with a mission.

They were going to locate this underground fight club and have a good time before he had to get serious and play the doting fiancé to Katharine Karak.

Car parked, he stared at the dated two-story hotel. It was tidy, but old. The lot probably hadn't seen a new layer of asphalt in a decade or more. "I'll get our room keys."

He left Jerry and Woods at the car and jogged toward the office. Inside, it smelled like preserved nicotine and old man. His eyes landed on the name tag of the shrunken form slumped on a lawn chair behind the counter. Carl. He sniffed again. Shifter.

Trent cleared his throat, trying to awaken the old guy without startling him into a heart attack. It took three tries before wrinkled eyelids cracked open.

He slowly straightened and said in a gravelly voice, "Didn't hear the bell."

Trent glanced back over the door. There indeed was a bell suspended above the door that sat at an awkward angle. He stepped over and gave it a knock, sending it jangling back into place.

Carl nodded his thanks with a grunt. "Reservations?"

Trent gave his name and listened to the short list of instructions. He leaned forward to receive the key, lowered his voice, and asked, "What kind of entertainment is there around here?"

With a key between his fingers, Carl's hand slowed on its way toward Trent's. "How'd you mean?" he asked, squinting at Trent.

"Oh, you know. My friend likes female company. And I like a little sport."

"Sport?"

Despite being alone in the cramped hotel office, Trent shrugged and whispered, "A little gaming."

"Gambling y'mean."

Trent nodded.

Carl leaned back, eyes narrowed on the younger man. "Female companions are scarce around this town if I'm knowing what you're meaning. And most folks go to the bigger cities for gambling, if I'm knowing your meaning there too. Otherwise, this town is simple. Most gather at the pub next door for a drink or two then go home." He placed the key on the counter.

"Bigger cities, huh? Like Vancouver? We just drove in from the airport there."

Carl shrugged. "Could be. I don't know nothing about those kinds of goings-on. I just know what's what here."

Trent nodded. "I see." But he wasn't quite sure he did. "Thanks for the room."

"Checkout's eleven."

"Got it." The doorbell jangled on his way out, and he sighed as he returned to the car.

"What's wrong?" Woods asked.

"Looks like we'll have to go all the way back to the city for a good time. Jerry, I thought you said the gaming was close to here." He scowled, pulling his bag from the trunk.

"My inquiries said that there was an established fight ring right in this area. In fact, rumor was that it was run by the notorious Terry family."

"Terry?" Woodrow said. "Isn't that the place we're going for your party?"

"You think they're the same family?"

Jerry shrugged. "How many Terry families do you think there are way the hell out here in Mountain-town-nowhere?"

"So, you're telling me, you think my future brother-in-law

is marrying into an illegal fight ring family? Ridiculous. Mrs. Karak would never allow that."

Jerry held up his hands. "Hey, man, I'm just recounting what I heard."

"Why didn't you mention any of this before?"

"You were both…busy, and any time I tried to bring up what I was finding, you weren't interested. Besides, I realized that if you knew of the connection, it might make you anxious before the party, and I didn't want your anxiety to flare up."

Trent frowned at his buddy. No, he didn't either. "You're always looking out for me—for both of us, Jerry. You're a great guy."

Jerry smiled his wide toothy smile. "Always. Let's dump our bags and check things out."

Bags in hand, Trent dropped the trunk lid of his rented Mercedes and led his friends to their room for the next few days.

I have the best of friends. Always looking out for me—for each other.

Because they had always had each other's backs since their college days.

He just wished Jerry wouldn't hold out on him sometimes.

Though it was usually for his own benefit in the end.

To protect him.

But he did like knowing stuff, too.

10

Katz rolled over, flattened palm batting at the alarm clock button.

She flopped back. Something hard was wedged between her ribs and the mattress. Flinging a hand behind herself, she shoved one of her favorite sex toys out of its offensive position and sighed, turning onto her side. Another peeked out from under the edge of the sheet.

"Useless. The lot of you," she snapped at them. There was a third one somewhere near her feet.

Memories of Zeek's display slammed her onto her back with a huff.

Asshole.

All night. All night she had replayed his words and his movements, his kiss, over and over in her head. Her body needed the explosive release that only he could provide. Her favorite toys held no comparison.

Asshole.

You deserved it, Katz.

Her conscience held no pity for her.

Quiet.

You know he cares about you. He knows you care about him.
Hush.
Your behavior was reproachable. You deserved to be tossed out by your scruff.

Katz rolled out of bed, slamming her feet down on the cold floor, shocking herself awake. She stomped around her bed, snatching up the collection of vibrators to dump in the bathroom for cleaning as her internal argument raged on.

... so self-centered.
I was thinking of him.
Really?
Best not to get involved like we did before. Better not to give him hope.
Is that right?
Yeah.

She set about cleaning up then preparing for her morning shower.

You're ridiculous.

The water streamed to life, flooding the tiled room with hot steam.

Stripping, she ignored the trailing words of her conscience as it became distracted by the soothing flow of water over her head and shoulders.

Silence.

Just the hiss of water.

After a luxurious, frothy cleansing, she stepped out, dressed, and strode for the coffee maker.

After coffee, she'd let her mind ruminate again.

Aromatic cup in hand, she leaned on the hard edge of the counter, staring at the opposite wall for a long moment before sipping the hot brew.

Moving into the living room, she stood in front of the large picture window of her guest house, studying the identical house across the path and its copies stretching out from either side. Her gaze locked on Zeek's front door as he appeared in sweats.

She watched, heart in her throat, as he turned to look in each direction. He drew his long blond hair into a ponytail behind his head, feet bouncing down the steps. He jogged right past her house without so much as a glance. She noted the little wireless earbuds as he passed.

She watched his smooth gait as he disappeared out of view.

What am I going to do?

Girl, you fucked this up. Bad.

Language!

Her inner kitty sniffed. *You deserve all the sharp words this time.*

"What's done is done," she said into her mug.

Apologize.

She sputtered her coffee.

No. Karaks don't apologize.

More bullshit. Do something. You have to work with this man.

I won't give in. I'm done giving in to everyone else's expectations. He expects me to crawl into bed with him.

Her parents expected her to work for the business, marry a mate of their choosing, and produce more heirs to keep their legacy going.

What about what I want?

What do you want?

I— I don't know.

Of course, you do.

She sighed, still staring in the direction Zeek had gone.

Zeek.

But not just Zeek. I want to show my mother I can run her company as well as she does. No. I want her to see how capable I am. No, that's not right either.

You want people to recognize your abilities and respect you.

Yes.

Not just as one of my mother's tools.

She giggled at herself.

I'm such a tool.

Did anyone even say that anymore?

Focus.

What do I want?

"Yes, I want Mummy to respect me. I want her to accept my choices—but she never will. Why should I get to choose my mate when no one other than Darcy was given that freedom?" she said aloud.

Thanks to you.

"No. I failed. I failed to achieve any real negotiation with Old Man Terry. And the only reason mother gave Darcy the go-ahead was because of Corra. Corra earned her respect."

Katz, you helped persuade her.

"Maybe. But it doesn't matter. It isn't enough. It's never enough."

Nothing I ever do is enough for her.

I'm *not enough for her.*

You're enough for Zeek. He knows it, you know it. Run away with him.

Katz snorted. After last night, that would never happen.

She gulped the remainder of her coffee, feeling worse than before her delicious shower.

This self-argument was going nowhere. At least she was keeping it quiet this time.

She grabbed her bag and headed for the classroom.

If she were as dedicated as she claimed, she'd throw all of herself into this work.

And she had said she was dedicated.

As she crossed the open green space toward the main building, Zeek jogged past her from behind, startling her.

He didn't acknowledge her or look back.

Her chest tightened.

Just another staff member.

Just another colleague, as she'd wanted.

Her heels tapped the paved path at an increased rate.

By the time Zeek arrived in the classroom, he discovered Katz had already planned out the lessons for the next two weeks. Part of him thought he should be annoyed she'd gone ahead and done it without consulting him, but he realized he really wasn't.

It was good that she was staying true to what she was there for.

No matter that he'd tried to derail both of them last night.

That had been a mistake. A big mistake.

She'd made it clear that she wanted to remain on professional terms.

He should have respected that.

He would respect that moving forward.

Especially now that they'd gotten out into the open what needed to be said.

They still desired one another. They still had obligations to fulfill.

She was practically engaged.

His gut tightened. His gorilla growled low in his throat.

Deep down, he'd known.

That was how the Karak family worked.

All arranged marriages for the benefit of the family business.

Acid rose up from his gut. He swallowed it down.

It wasn't too different from how his family had operated. Until his father and grandfather had been incarcerated and his mother had taken over running things on the estate.

She kept pressuring him to do it. Run things.

It's not my place. It never was.

Caleb should be running the family estate. He was always meant to.

Caleb never wanted it.

I did. At one time.

Nah, I'm done with all that now. Mom can handle it. She should be the one to take over. She deserves it and would do things right.

He just needed to figure out how to secure it for her. Ensure that no one could ever take it from her. That his grandfather's long reach couldn't send it all crashing down the mountainside out of spite. As he had no doubt that he would do.

He glanced at Katz again, working at her laptop, ignoring his presence as he unpacked his bag.

She'd asked him to set up the meeting to negotiate with his grandfather. He'd been present when she'd argued Corra and Darcy's case and how well the two families would complement one another under certain circumstances.

He'd had to admit she'd been pretty damned ballsy in her approach. Head high, determination unwavering, sound proposal. He just needed to take the family business to the right side of the legal line by propping up their current strengths.

Bold. Beautiful. The proposal had detailed exactly how he could do that.

He'd never ever seen anyone have the cheek to propose to a family deeply rooted in illegal activity that they should change that.

She'd done it for her brother—so that he could be happy.

Katz had it in her to lead her mother's company, if not on her own then certainly with the elder brother that was already serving on the board, as Darcy was supposed to have done. Zeek had learned all this during their previous time together when Katz was hatching her plan of approach.

He studied her as she worked. A frown wrinkled her forehead.

She doesn't know how brilliant she is.

She could do anything she set her mind to.

If only she'd shake off her mother's leash.

Zeek knew what it was like, living at the direction of someone else.

And he'd hated it.

Katz had indirectly prompted him to change.

He leaned on the table, looking across the room at her.

"Have you ever thought of building your own company?"

"Excuse me?" She looked up from beneath her furrowed brow.

"Start your own company. Run it yourself?"

"Are you smoking again?" she demanded, left brow lifted.

He jerked upright. "No. Not in a long time."

Her right brow rose to meet the other.

"Not since the last time we smoked together."

Before everything went to shit.

She dropped her gaze back to her laptop. "Good. And no. I have no plans to start my own business. Why would I?"

"You'd be amazing at it."

She looked up again. Her expression softened. "Thanks, but no. I'm committed to my family's business."

He shrugged.

"What about you? You could take over your grandfather's business."

He laughed. "No."

"Why not? You're just as capable."

"Based on what? The multitude of grunt errands he used to send me on?"

"You know more than you give yourself credit for."

He shook his head. "Mom is trying to push me into taking over. I don't want it."

She sat up straighter. "I thought you did. I thought you wanted to take over along with Caleb?"

"At one time, maybe. He's the rightful heir to the estate."

"He made it very clear he doesn't want it. From what I've seen and heard, he's very dedicated to the Furry United Coalition."

"Mom can do it," he said again. "I just have to figure out how to secure it for her.

Katz' expression changed again. "She should seek counsel on what her rights are to the estate, given the situation."

"She won't be talking to the *family* lawyer, that's for sure. He's been let go. I'll talk to her about it. She's struggling to get the taxes and utilities paid after all the renovations, so right now, she's trying to figure out how to increase revenue. Whatever grandfather did, she had no part in it, so I'd imagine that side of his business is in turmoil. I don't care."

Katz nodded. "We briefly spoke on the matter and agreed to work on it after the engagement party. It will take time, but she can build something out of all this."

"I hope so." Would it be enough? Soon enough? He just hoped it didn't take so long she lost everything.

The sounds of doors banging and shuffling alerted them to the arrival of their students.

"We can talk more about this later." She hesitated. "If you want. We can meet in the cafeteria."

Neutral ground.

He nodded, and they both turned their attention to final preparations before classes began.

11

During Katz' break, she found a message from Darcy on her phone asking her to meet him.

She called his cell, and he picked up on the first ring.

"Katz, hey, thanks for calling back so soon. I have a favor to ask."

"I don't have any shoe polish at the Academy, but I do have hair product you can borrow."

"Nothing like that. I need you to go to dinner with me in the city."

"The city? Why?"

"I need your brain."

She laughed. "Shopping for the party?"

"Yeeah... Good idea. We can find me a suit for the party. When do your classes finish? I'll pick you up."

She told him what time she'd meet him in the Academy lot.

The cafeteria meeting with Zeek would have to wait.

Darcy picked Katz up at the allotted time. They drove to the city and not only found a quality suit for him but a party dress and shoes for herself. Now it was dinner time and Katz was famished after all that shopping.

The maître d' led them toward a table with a breathtaking view of the harbor.

"We'll take that one," Darcy said, gesturing toward a table set away from the floor-to-ceiling windows and at the back of the room.

Despite the restaurant not having a bad seat in the house, this particular one was most certainly the least desirable.

"But—" Katz started.

"This one, please," Darcy insisted.

The maître d' nodded and settled them in. Darcy pulled a chair for Katz then took his own seat. Both were positioned to see the entire room at a glance.

Katz lay her napkin across her lap as she assessed her brother, who scanned the other diners.

No one went to a premier restaurant to sit in the corner.

"Who are we spying on?"

His gaze shot back to her face.

She watched his expressions, as he clearly hadn't expected her to call him out.

He frowned as he decided what exactly to tell her. Finally he shrugged and grinned. "Some big shots I'm hoping you can identify for me. On the down low, of course."

"Of course. You're paying. I'll have the best escargot on the menu."

He flinched but agreed. He was on agent income now and no longer accessed the Karak fortune anytime he wanted.

"This is the part of my brain you actually wanted." A thrill of excitement fluttered through her belly.

He nodded, sipping his water with another glance across the vast room as a large party settled at a table by the windows.

She sniffed. Shifters. All at angles that obscured their faces from her view, as they mostly faced the windows.

Darcy was momentarily distracted when their waiter arrived to take their order then returned with a bottle of wine.

"I haven't seen you this tense since you brought Corra to meet our family."

He picked up his wine glass then held it aloft. "To you."

She laughed. "To me? Whatever for? You're the one getting engaged." She lifted her glass to his, and they both sipped.

He shrugged, visibly forcing himself to relax. "Just for being you. I appreciate that you talked Mother into backing off on her marriage plans so that Corra and I could be together. And Corra appreciates that you're planning to help her aunt with her business. We both know mother is dictating the party plans, but we both appreciate that you're doing all of that as well—on top of your job at the Academy. You're amazing, little sister."

Katz flushed at her brother's acknowledgments. "All in a day's work." She winked, seeing the unguarded happiness in his eyes at the mention of Corra.

No, she would never, ever, tell him how the negotiations with their mother actually went.

"It pleases me to see you so happy," she said. "You've worked hard to be where you are."

"I am and never thought I would be. Truly."

Her heart swelled. She reached across the table and squeezed his hand.

The appetizers arrived.

"Mmm, these are so good. You have to try some." Katz dipped the triangle of fluffy bread into the well of garlic butter her escargot were in.

"The acoustics in this place are terrible. I can't hear anything they're talking about."

"What do you expect in a quality restaurant, Darcy?" She rolled her eyes. "They're the ones you're scoping?"

He nodded. "Some."

With a quick glance to ensure no one was close by, she spoke into her napkin so that only Darcy would hear. "What exactly is it you need?"

He reached for an escargot. "Connections to an event slated for tonight," he said before popping it into his mouth. "You're right. These are fantastic."

"And?" she prompted.

"That's it. I just need to know who is who."

"Well then, let's go to this event."

"Absolutely not." His voice rose.

She blinked at him, pointedly raising her glass as several diners turned curious glances in their direction.

"Erm. This dinner is on me," he said, voice still raised.

"Oh, come on," she whispered, leaning toward him. "I've never been to an illegal fight ring, Darcy. That's what this is, right? For your case?"

"And you never will," he whispered back. "And yes, it is so behave yourself."

They pulled away from one another when their meals were placed in front of them.

Katz dug into her steak, chewing.

"What's wrong with your food?" Darcy asked.

"Nothing. Why?"

"You're frowning at it."

She waved in dismissal. "Nothing, really. Just not as good as Zeek's steak is all."

Darcy's brow shot up. "Oh? Do tell."

She flushed again. "Nothing to tell. We're work colleagues and had dinner one evening, is all." She suppressed the memory of everything that followed the steak.

"Colleagues, huh?" His gaze turned suspicious. "I remember

how you looked at him that first night you saw him at The Hub."

Katz burst out laughing. "You don't!"

"Your eyes were glued to his ass, Katz." Darcy shuddered. "I can't unsee the expression on your face, as much as I wish I could."

She quickly sipped her drink, trying to think of some other conversational topic before Darcy's brain went where it shouldn't.

"Mom would disapprove."

"Who I do or do not date is no one's business."

Darcy laughed. "Bravo, little sister. I sincerely hope that's true." He smiled at her, affection filling his eyes.

A loud guffaw drew her attention to the table of shifters Darcy had been watching.

I know that laugh.

They both turned their attention to the rising noise from that direction. An older man with a graying circular hairline stood, pretending to throw punches at a much younger man, who looked as though he'd spent a lifetime clutching a jackhammer.

Handsome, clothes fit nice, not as tall as Zeek, nor was his hair as long or glorious. It was shaved so close that his scalp gleamed as much as the older man's did under the restaurant's amber lighting.

"Here, take my picture," Darcy said, shoving his phone at Katz before switching seats so that he was between her and the group. "Get those guys in the background."

She did, ensuring she got as many of the diners in the shots as possible.

Darcy returned to his original seat.

"He's a fighter?"

"Could be. I'll have to get Caleb and Zeek to ID him. Do you recognize any of the others?"

"I recognized that laugh, but I haven't pinned his face yet. Those loud, obnoxious *old boys* all blend together over the years." She studied the group a moment longer then asked casually, "Zeek is helping you too?"

"We need all the help we can get if we're going to see some results soon."

"I think I remember where I saw him before. Do you remember the Aslans?"

"Trent's family? How can I forget? Have you wriggled out of that contract yet?"

"Yes, Trent's family, and no. Anyway, I'm sure that guy with the laugh was at a couple of parties Mom hosted, along with the Aslans, a few months ago."

"Name?"

"Give me a few more minutes and it will come to me."

"Sure. I'm going to the men's room."

She nodded, not taking her eyes off their targets for a full minute. Then, with a quick glance to ensure Darcy was out of sight, she rose from her chair and approached the table, subtly adjusting her clothing and hair as she walked to ensure they highlighted particular aspects of her figure.

The conversation trailed to a stop at her approach.

"Gentlemen, good evening." She beamed at them, the one she recognized now as a major portfolio investor that attended several of the parties her mother organized in particular. "Mr. Harper, I just wanted to say hello and ask after your wife. How is Mrs. Harper?"

"Divorced. Join us?"

"Oh, I wouldn't want to interrupt your gentlemen's evening out any further. I'm dining with my brother in celebration of his engagement." She placed a hand to her chest, widening her smile. "So sweet of you to offer."

Several hushed comments and jokes about marriage ensued with good-natured laughter.

"Well, congratulate him for us and tell him to have all the fun he can get before he's married, because once he is…" Mr. Harper shrugged with a grin, his beady blue eyes intense as they narrowed on her, flicking up and down her figure.

"Oh, I will. Do you have any suggestions for him? I would like to do something fun with him before marital responsibilities take him over." She laughed, patting him on the shoulder.

Mr. Harper glanced around the table at his guests, landing on the young man he'd been play-fighting with. "Does your brother enjoy good sport?"

Katz shrugged, deciding obtuse was a good option here. "Don't all males? Ah, there he is now. Darcy!" She waved him over.

Seeing her, he quickly schooled his frown into mild curiosity and approached the table.

"This is my brother, Darcy Karak," she said to the table in general.

"Steve Harper." The older man introduced himself to Darcy. "Your lovely sister here says you're getting married and need a little fun before life as you know it ends. We have just the thing for you. Tonight, in fact." Harper clamped a large hand on Darcy's shoulder and gave him a friendly shake.

"Oh, I wouldn't want to impose on your plans, but I appreciate the invitation all the same. Katz and I should be going." He sent her a pointed look, his lips tight.

"Nonsense! Your mother hosted many entertaining parties on our behalf. The least I can do is take her cubs out for a good time."

Uh-oh. Darcy is pissed I'm involved.

She shrugged and tossed a curl over her shoulder, offering a helpless grin. He'd said he wanted identities. Well, here was his chance.

"Mr. Harper said something about good sports."

"Sports, huh?" Darcy turned his attention back to the rest of the suits at the table, extending his hand, making introductions.

Here we go.

She studied each of the faces, trying to remember defining features and scents for later recall. Mr. Harper—a crane. The fighter smelled like a fisher but not quite. A bear, two wolves, an eagle, and a weasel who watched her far too intently.

She suppressed a shudder, maintaining her smile as the men chatted amongst themselves.

"Where is the event being held so we can meet you there?" Darcy prompted.

"Don't worry about that. You'll ride with me. It's not every day one hosts a Karak to a sort-of public event." He chuckled, leaning in close to Katz as he whispered with a tip of his head, "I'm all about the bragging rights."

Belatedly, consequences filtered into Katz' brain.

Public event.

Karaks at a public event. If this indeed was an illegal fight ring and not one but *two* Karaks were present, others would surely find out.

Maybe if they were careful and kept to themselves, they could remain anonymous.

Harper picked up his discarded jacket, flagging the server. "I'll introduce you to everyone."

She gulped.

"Sure," Darcy said, voice light. "I'll just call my future brother-in-law to let him know I won't be meeting him for drinks tonight and settle our bill."

Darcy's hand gripped Katz' elbow as he steered her back toward their table where his own jacket and her purse remained. "What the hell did you just do?" he hissed in her ear.

"What you asked me to do. I'm helping."

"Not. Like. This," he growled, took his phone from his

jacket pocket, and dialed Caleb's number. "Mom is going to maul me."

"Katz did *what* now?" Caleb barked, drawing Zeek's attention from the files he'd been looking over. "I see. You have your receiver on? Good. Text me the location once you're there. I'm leaving now to provide backup... Like hell you don't, Darcy. You're not going into an illegal fight ring with only your sister."

"He can't take Katz to a fight. What the hell is he thinking?" Zeek snarled at Caleb, who held up a hand to halt any further tirades.

"Yes, well, it will take me some time to get there, but I will be there. Don't do anything stupid without me."

"Us. I'm going with you," Zeek said, heart pounding.

Caleb lifted a brow. "Thought you didn't want to get involved any more than was necessary?"

"Your fancy-shoed partner will get his expensive suit-covered ass handed to him if he looks at anyone the wrong way. How the hell did he even find a way into a fight in the first place?"

"Katz."

"Uhm...?"

Caleb shrugged. "No time for details. Can I borrow your truck?"

"No. I'm driving."

"Why the sudden turn-around on this? I thought these files were as deep as your involvement went." Caleb grabbed his coat, following Zeek out of his campus home where they'd met to review the case file.

They jogged toward the lot, Zeek leading the way, ignoring Caleb's questions.

They got into the truck, and Zeek started it and threw it into gear. "Where are they?"

"The city."

Zeek swallowed. Long drive. It would be forever before he got there to get her out again. His foot hit the gas, and they sped out of the parking lot toward the main road, tires squealing on the tarmac.

Caleb gripped the holy-shit handle, eyes wide as he stared at his cousin.

As soon as the truck finished fishtailing and settled into a steady speed, which was well above the limit and unsafe for such winding mountain roads, Caleb settled on his seat, eyes still glued to Zeek.

"What?"

Caleb smirked. "I'm sure Darcy will be fine. You don't have to kill the transmission trying to bury the needle in the red."

"Yeah, I'm sure he will be," Zeek snarled.

Caleb laughed. He threw back his head and laughed some more.

"What?" Zeek didn't take his eyes off the road.

"You." Caleb laughed harder. "I've never seen you like this. Ever." He wiped his eyes.

"What are you talking about?"

"You're worse than I was. Man, you've got it bad. And for Katz? Despite Darcy's efforts to be at the top of everyone's list, I'm sure it's not him you're driving the truck to ruin for right now, is he?"

"I don't know what you're talking about," Zeek muttered, heat flooding his cheeks. His foot eased off the gas so that they were no longer at warp speed on the narrow road.

"I *know* you, Zeek."

Zeek wanted to swipe the annoying grin off his cousin's face but didn't want to risk swerving off the side of the mountain just to satisfy the urge. If they survived, his truck would be trashed and of no use to get him closer to Katz. However, it *would* get them down the mountain faster, and then they could just hitch a ride…

What the hell am I thinking?

He blinked. *Calm yourself.*

He sucked air into his lungs, forcing his pulse to a reasonable rate, and chose to ignore Caleb's questions and comments.

"Plug the address into the GPS."

Caleb checked his phone then added the location to the navigation system.

"Fuck," Zeek said after glancing at the pin on the map. "Fuck." His hands slammed the steering wheel.

"What?"

"That's one of Garcia's sites."

"Fuck," Caleb said.

"Yeah." Zeek's foot pressed the gas pedal down again. Caleb tightened his grip on the handle above his head.

12

Katz couldn't look, and she couldn't *not* look.

Her fingernails clawed her brother's arm as they sat watching the brutal mess below them, surrounded by a wire fence. Everyone around them cheered, booed, screamed, and shouted.

Including Harper and his cronies, who sat on her other side.

The young man from the dinner was indeed a fisher. More than, really. But not in a way she could describe. He was huge, with razor claws and teeth.

Not natural.

She continued to stare until she finally tore her eyes from the desecration that was a fight ring. She looked to Darcy, who watched stone-faced.

He wouldn't look at her.

Mother would kill him if she found out they were here. Then she would kill Katz for recklessly jeopardizing their reputation. She would never respect her now. Katz would be forever designated to head the HR department in the company. There was no way she'd be allowed in the boardroom with their elder brother.

She glanced at Darcy again.

He needed help for his case. It's important.

If anything went wrong, she'd just have to spin it to their advantage—whatever that was.

By now, the pummeled loser was cleared from the ring and the blood was being cleaned up in preparation for the next fight.

This was nothing like the few professional fighting sports she'd been to in the past. This was ruthless.

Are there even any rules?

I don't like this.

She didn't like the violence on display, but she also didn't like the kernel of truth about the suppressed side of herself.

Part of her reacted to the violence on a primal level. It riled her blood, encouraging her to hiss and spit, to bare tooth and claw and jump into the fray. Her person-brain reasoned that this was in no way a hunt. It was pure violence for the sake of violence.

Zeek's grandfather used to force him and Caleb into these fights?

She shuddered.

"Come with me. I want you to meet someone before the next fight starts." Harper stood then leaned close to Katz. Too close. His gaze felt like oil sliding up and down her body as he extended a hand to help her up.

On her other side, Darcy's growl was a low warning.

Ignoring Darcy, she tossed a curl over her shoulder, smiled, and accepted Harper's hand as she stood then quickly slid her fingers away. "Another fighter? Isn't this exciting, Darcy?"

Darcy stood, shadowing her. "Very."

"No, my dear. Not a fighter. The owner of the venue. Very important man."

Darcy's usually fluid posture went rigid next to her.

"Really?" she asked, breathless and wide-eyed while her

fingers grazed her chest. "I love knowing all of the important people."

"Like your mother, I'm sure," Harper murmured, eyes following her hand.

"Of course!" She smiled. "I have to be on the lookout for all the best folks to invite to Mummy's parties, right?" She scrunched her nose as she tipped her shoulder coyly.

The much-older man chuckled. To Darcy he said, "Your sister is a delight. I may just steal her from you."

She glanced at Darcy's murderous expression and hissed. "You're supposed to be suave and carefree."

Which she was sure he'd be pulling off flawlessly if she weren't involved. But she was, so he needed to adjust and remember his training.

Katz was just doing as she always did, at every party or function her mother dragged her to—playing the whimsical socialite to collect information. This was no different.

She thought of Zeek's class and what they'd told the students. Power structures. Hierarchies.

As her gaze slid around the venue, she noticed that the weasel in Harper's group, which she'd forgotten about, now followed them.

Harper presented Katz and Darcy to a man seated among a group of men and women, all expensively dressed. Many accessorized with weapons.

Weapons were never, ever allowed in her mother's functions. Only their own security was ever armed. She swallowed.

Darcy's light touch on her back gave her some comfort as he leaned toward the man Harper introduced them to.

Phil Garcia regarded them with mild curiosity a moment before his grin widened beneath his thick black handlebar mustache. "The socialite and the playboy." He laughed, shaking Darcy's hand, and then he pulled Katz' fingers to his lips.

She resisted the urge to wipe her hand on her skirt as soon as he released it.

From the corner of her eye, she noted that the weasel hovered nearby but didn't engage during introductions.

Who is this guy, and what is he after?

There was no time to think about the little man anymore. Garcia was turning out to be quite chatty—and knowledgeable about her family.

He and Harper were talking openly about her mother's business and her connections.

"Since I'm hosting the Karak cubs, I'm sure your mother will reciprocate and host me at one of her famous parties," Garcia said.

She gulped.

"I will certainly relay what a gracious host you are," Katz assured him.

I'm in over my head. This was a mistake. Dear Isis, how do I get us out of this?

Panic was riding up her esophagus when the tone of the waiting crowd shifted.

Garcia's attention turned away from Katz and Darcy to see what the audience was murmuring about.

Katz' breath caught in her throat.

Zeek and Caleb stood by the door, looking in their direction.

Garcia chuckled. The sound ricocheted up Katz' spine, chilling her blood.

Zeek ripped the steel door of Garcia's place open and strode inside, Caleb two steps behind.

He wanted to go in there, punch Garcia in the face, grab Katz, and get out. And maybe punch Garcia in the face a couple more times.

Oily, manipulative, domineering, and underhanded.

Zeek certainly despised the man for all that had transpired in the past but more so for his behavior toward his mother very recently.

He'd sent his men to shake her up and try to force her to work with him.

His grandfather's most-hated rival.

This was dangerous.

Dangerous for them to be there.

Dangerous for Katz and Darcy.

Garcia was predictably unpredictable. Like Old Man Terry.

Did as he pleased, expected anything he wanted, and had no qualms about meting out his own idea of consequences to anyone that opposed him.

So far, he was being gentle with Sheila.

The Old Man was still alive—for now—and capable of getting word out if needed.

No one knew that Zeek had been part of his grandfather's downfall. It wasn't the sort of thing one broadcasted, unless it was a power play.

Which it wasn't.

"Zeek." Caleb's harsh whisper reminded him to be cautious.

"I know," he said to Caleb. A lot was riding on what happened in the next hour.

How was Garcia going to view their sudden appearance in his place?

"This is about Mom," Zeek said.

Caleb nodded as he slid in front of Zeek and led the way toward Garcia.

"Ignore her," Caleb murmured—meaning Katz.

Zeek ground his teeth as he scanned the faces of everyone seated in Garcia's vicinity.

How the hell did Katz and Darcy get themselves into his circle so damned fast?

Zeek heard Katz' elevated voice.

"Mr. Garcia, thank you for your hospitality, but I do need to be going. I have so much to do tomorrow."

Garcia's gaze was glued to Caleb's and Zeek's approach. "You should stay, Ms. Karak. Perhaps you can help me persuade Mr. LeBrute to fight for me this evening. He's one of the finest fighters I've ever seen in the ring."

Zeek and Caleb now stood at the edge of Garcia's cluster of tables. His men were a barrier around him.

Zeek clenched his fists. His gorilla huffed, seeing that his kitty was on the wrong side of the barrier and chafed at the need for caution.

"Perhaps another time? I will be speaking to my mother in the morning. I will tell her all about you." Katz gave Garcia a wide smile. Darcy shook the man's hand.

Everyone's attention was on Zeek and Caleb.

The Karak siblings had barely turned away when Garcia addressed Caleb. "The prodigal grandson. Returning to the ring, are you?"

"I'm here to tell you to stop harassing my mother," Zeek cut in, drawing Garcia's attention and getting to the point.

Garcia shrugged. "Not harassment. Just an invitation to work with me or, at the very least, put in a good word for me now that your grandfather is in prison." He grinned. "I just offered to take her fighters off her hands for her. They can train here. Practice for the big league."

Katz and Darcy slipped away.

"My aunt is off-limits. Deal with us," Caleb said to Garcia.

Garcia moved toward Caleb, but his gaze flicked toward Zeek. "Perhaps I will do business with you instead. Work with me. Your family has always had such a high standard for training. Help my fighters see their full potential."

"We'll think about it," Caleb said.

Garcia turned his attention to Zeek. "I saw how the crowd turned its eye on you when you walked through that door. They remember. You have a lot of sway in this world."

Zeek couldn't deny the pull of the power—the energy of the crowd. The memory of how it felt to be in that ring. Better than anything else. A drug. "I don't fight anymore."

The noise in the venue rose, and the announcer called out the names of the next fighters.

"Pity." Garcia eyed him then turned back to Caleb. "I'm sure I can find some way to convince you both to work with me. Don't worry. I will reach out." He turned his back on them, returning to his seat, attention on the ring.

Zeek cast another glance around the spectators. Everyone's attention was now on the ring and the fighters making their way into it.

He didn't look at it, or anyone else, as he led the way back out of the venue.

13

Katz and Darcy hailed a taxi.

For the entire ride back to the restaurant, her tummy was in knots.

Darcy was silent.

She bit her lip, thinking of something to say to ease the tension. She had nothing that could make it better.

She couldn't even push an apology through her larynx.

Her instinct had guided her actions, and she couldn't be sorry for it. That was one thing her mother had always preached in business. Follow your instincts.

Katz just wished she was permitted to follow her instincts in other aspects of her life.

Shunting that thought aside, she returned her focus to her very angry brother.

His phone buzzed. After a moment, he pulled it from his pocket, read the message, and replaced it without a word to Katz.

Her manicured fingernails tapped her purse, set on her lap, until they arrived back at the restaurant where they'd left Darcy's car.

In his car, the silence continued.

Katz hated it. She always had. This was Darcy's way, until he was calm enough to speak.

He navigated the car out of the downtown core, bypassing the entrance to the highway.

Katz turned her attention to him, curious. But under the continued silence, he offered no explanation, just drove. She sighed, watching the dark landscape rush past them.

Minutes later, he turned into an empty ocean-view lookout.

She recognized Zeek's truck. He and Caleb were visible inside the cab as she and Darcy pulled up next to them.

Darcy barely had the car in Park when Zeek appeared to haul him out of the vehicle, fists buried in Darcy's lapels. "What the fuck were you thinking bringing her in there, Karak?"

"Zeek—" Caleb barked.

"Shut up, Caleb," Zeek spat. "Neither of us should have been there. I told you I didn't want to get involved, and you sure as fuck shouldn't have dragged *her* into this."

Darcy's hands clamped on Zeek's substantially larger wrists, somehow managing to break Zeek's hold on his jacket. Darcy was a tall man, but Zeek overshadowed both him and Caleb with his size.

"What I do with my sister is none of your fucking business, Zeek. And as far as *I'm* concerned, helping us shut these fuckers down is the least you can do. You owe Corra that much," Darcy snarled up into Zeek's face.

Zeek's jaw clenched as he glared at Darcy. "You're right. I *do* owe her. But that doesn't excuse *you* for taking Katz into that place."

"Zeek, he couldn't have known how dangerous Garcia is," Caleb said, voice low.

"You should have told him," Zeek spat at Caleb.

Katz' heart hammered, watching the exchange between her

brother and her former lover. She'd never, ever seen either of them like this.

She inserted herself into the narrow space between them. She made eye contact with Zeek first. "Thank you for your concern, but as you can see, I'm safe. We're both safe."

Zeek snorted, but his posture visibly relaxed several degrees.

She turned to Darcy. "I followed my instinct, exactly as Mother taught us to do when it comes to business, and let things play out."

"It was dangerous," he said, echoing Zeek's sentiment. "You know there will be consequences. Dinner and a bit of surveillance, Katz. That's all it was supposed to be. Instead, you got us into—"

"Into the venue and the presence of the man you needed access to."

"He's right, Katz," Caleb said. "There will be consequences."

"Mother will go ballistic when she finds out," Darcy warned her unnecessarily.

"Garcia is going to lean even harder on Zeek and Aunt Sheila. And by extension, Corra."

"Don't worry about me," Zeek said.

"Look, you got the IDs you asked for, and more," she pointed out.

Darcy blew out a pent-up breath and scrubbed his hands over his face. "Yes, we did," he finally said. "I'll take my receiver to Suricatta in the morning to go over what we've got."

Caleb checked his watch. "Suricatta stays up late. We should go now and figure out what our next move in the morning is when we meet with Miranda and Chase."

Katz barely heard them discussing possibilities. Her attention was on Zeek's face. His concerned gaze returned to her face over and over. She hadn't seen him that agitated since the night FUC arrested his grandfather. Granted, she'd been locked in another room with armed guards when things started getting messy.

"Katz? We have to get this material back to the Academy," Darcy said.

"Zeek, do you mind driving me back?" she asked.

His eyes shot to her face. He gave a sharp nod, then another. "Yeah, I'll see you home safe."

She turned to her brother and Caleb. "You two go ahead. I'm sure there's something important recorded on Darcy's device. What is it anyway? A pen? A button? You don't smoke, so it can't be a lighter." She grinned at him.

"Joe's latest tech is smaller than that." He tapped his ear lobe where a small stud she hadn't paid attention to before glittered under the moonlight. "Bear tested it out during his trip to Hong Kong. He swears it works great."

"Huh. Cool." She squeezed his arm. "Zeek will see me home. Go do your job, Darcy."

She'd sacrificed everything so he would be free to do the job he'd fought for—and have Corra in his life.

He pulled her into his arms, giving her a gruff hug. "Thanks for your help. I was just scared."

She squeezed him. "I know." She released him and watched as he and Caleb got into the car and drove off, leaving her alone with Zeek.

14

As soon as Darcy's car was out of sight, Katz found herself crushed to Zeek's chest, his fingers threaded through her hair and her lips opening to his.

It happened so fast she reeled under the urgency of his kiss, her hands pressed to his chest. She meant to push him away, but her head swarmed with his scent and her knees began to liquefy, causing her to lean farther into him.

Instead, her arms wound around his waist, pulling him impossibly closer as she stood on tiptoe to deepen their kiss.

Why was she trying to push him away? Oh, right. Obligations. Expectations.

Obligations she'd never wanted.

Fuck obligations and expectations. They were suffocating her.

Zeek was the air she breathed. From the start.

Instinct wasn't just for business situations. Or surveillance situations.

It was also for situations of the heart, and her instinct had been driving her into Zeek's arms since the first moment they met. The night she arrived to talk Darcy into agreeing with their parents' marriage contract.

Just like the one she promised to honor—no matter what.

Obligations…

She broke the kiss.

"Zeek…" His name caught in her throat.

"I know, Katz," he whispered against her lips. "I can't have you."

The sensation of his warm arms around her felt like the rightest thing in the world.

Sweet Isis, she could stay just like this forever. In Zeek's arms, under the light of the moon overlooking the Pacific Ocean, the Rocky Mountains at their backs.

She leaned back to look up at him.

His soulful eyes caressed her face.

Her heart swelled when he looked at her like that.

His gaze dropped to her lips.

Her nether regions reacted to the desire, clear in his expression.

She licked her lips.

"You shouldn't do that, Katz."

"Do what?"

"Entice me like that when you're forbidden fruit."

"Not forbidden yet. Technically, nothing is official until it's public. Like Darcy and Corra's engagement party."

"So, we still have a little time left."

Before I lose you forever.

She nodded, taking his large hand in hers, led him to his truck, and opened the door to the back seat. They both got in, and she immediately crawled into his lap and pulled the door closed.

The space was cramped and uncomfortable.

She didn't care.

It was perfect as she stared into Zeek's handsome face.

Anywhere with *him* was perfect.

Because I love you.

Her eyes drank his features into her memory greedily.

How could I have ever called you a distraction?

She knew her words had hurt him. Otherwise, he wouldn't have reacted the way he had that night.

And what a display it had been!

A smile teased her lips.

She wriggled her feet, letting the pumps thump to the floor as she settled into a better position to straddle Zeek's muscular legs.

"Are you sure you want to do this?" Zeek's gruff voice sent a shiver of longing up her spine.

"Are you, Zeek? After what I said?"

"At least now I know why…" He swallowed.

"Why I didn't reach out after… after that night?"

He nodded. "You should have told me."

"Yes, I should have but didn't know how." Her hands roamed over his shoulders, flitting and touching him.

His large hands left swaths of warmth in their wake as they, too, roamed her body, massaging her thighs and hips, sliding up and down her back.

Committing each other to memory—in case they might someday forget.

It wasn't just desire. It was so much more.

More that couldn't be.

Forbidden—as Zeek had said.

She'd been foolish to deny herself—both of them—that little bit of time left.

But was it fair? To re-establish something that couldn't be?

Was it fair to admit to him—to herself—what she felt? What he might feel?

Or was it just masochistic to unlock the final door to her heart?

"It's not enough," she whispered.

"We could get a room or go to my place," he said, searching her face.

"I mean this little bit of time. It isn't enough."

He started to speak again, but she devoured his words with a kiss, which he immediately deepened, reaching into her soul to draw her out.

She whimpered. Needing to feel more of his skin, she tugged at his shirt while he unzipped the back of her dress, pulling it down to bare her lace-and-silk bra. Finally, freeing him of his shirt, she let it drop to the seat next to him then leaned so that her breasts pressed to his chest, her arms encircling his shoulders.

She lay her head on his shoulder, nuzzled his neck, and breathed a deep sigh.

His hands stroked up and down her back, providing whatever comfort she needed in that moment. She allowed herself to relax into him for a few minutes longer, and then her lips grazed along the taut muscles of his throat, nipping and licking until she reached his ear lobe and gave it a little tug.

He chuckled. "You're sure you want to do this, kitten? You put an awful lot of effort into avoiding it."

"A foolish waste of time," she whispered into his ear. "I want you, Zeek."

Zeek's hands gripped her hips, lifting, as he shifted his forward toward the edge of the seat.

She reached down to unbuckle his belt, release the button on his jeans, and ease the zipper down, and then she slipped her hand behind the barrier of his boxers.

His lips found hers as she gripped his erection, stroking and massaging, while his hands found her heated center. Pushing aside the fragile fabric, his fingers delved and explored with as much deliberation as hers.

The gentle movements wound her tighter and tighter.

Sensing her need, he extracted his fingers so they could both discard the rest of their clothing. Zeek extracted a condom from his wallet, and she helped roll it onto him.

Katz atop Zeek, she looked down into his eyes, hooded with desire as he stared up into hers.

She dropped her gaze to his erection resting against her belly.

She needed him inside of her.

"I'm all yours, kitten. Only yours."

Her eyes met his. She swallowed past a lump that suddenly thickened her throat.

Rising up, she aligned her entrance to his tip. Holding his gaze, she slid down until he filled her.

Her breaths came in short gasps. "Oh, sweet Isis, I'm yours too, Zeek. Always have been."

His fingers gripped her hips as he shoved himself higher—deeper inside of her, forcing her to cry out.

She was atop him, but he held her fast, setting the pace and rhythm. Her mouth met his, their tongues mingling and swiping in countermeasure to the thrusting and grinding of their hips.

And when she reached her tipping point, he would slow the pace and tease her out, bringing her down again, only to push her to the precipice again and again until she lost all balance and toppled over the edge, taking him with her.

They fell fast and crashed hard.

She lay her head on his shoulder while they caught their breath, hearts pounding erratically, his body still held captive within hers.

Still semi-aroused, despite their dramatic climaxes.

She wasn't done with him yet.

They had a lot of catching up to do.

She sat up so that she could look down into his sated face. A mischievous grin tugged at her lips, and she gave her hips a little wriggle.

Zeek chuckled, deep in his chest as he dropped his head back on the headrest behind him. "Five more minutes, kitten. Just five more minutes."

She ignored his plea and began her second assault on his senses, licking, nibbling, and wriggling until he rose to meet her again.

Zeek's breath disappeared as he opened his eyes to stare up into Katz' passion-filled face. Crammed in the backseat of his truck, perched on his lap, she was a goddess.

Her parted swollen lips quirked at the corner with satisfaction. Her thick, silky hair tumbled over her shoulders. He couldn't resist running his fingers through it.

Their breaths puffed into each other's faces, reminding him that they were still connected to one another in breath and body.

Her fingers released the back of the seat behind his head, drifting through his hair to caress his cheeks. She leaned forward to brush her lips over his, stealing his breath again as her hands continued to drift until they found his, still clasped to her hips.

Lacing her fingers through his, as she'd done so many times in the past, she brought his left palm to her chest, placing it flat against the bare skin over the rapid beat of her heart.

He stared at their hands on her chest for a full minute as their breathing returned to normal after their shared ecstasy, just feeling it. Feeling her heart under his palm, skittering. The intimacy of the moment wrenched his own heart.

He glanced up into her gold-green eyes, full of unshed tears. Her lips tightened, but she said nothing.

She'd called him a distraction.

A necessary lie.

He swallowed the rising emotion.

Her body always told him that she wanted him.

His hand slid up her chest to her throat, drifting along her jaw.

She closed her eyes, pressing her cheek to his palm, nuzzling.

Her lips remained compressed against any words she might have uttered.

His thumb trailed along her closed mouth as he pulled her close again.

Her brows were furrowed. Droplets clung to her spiked lashes.

"It's okay," he whispered, not knowing exactly why but knowing that she needed to hear those words. Both thoroughly spent now, there were only words left to give. "Always."

Even when he had to give her up to the man her parents chose for her.

And she would uphold the agreement. For them. For her brother. No matter what it cost her.

Was there any way *he* could make himself a more desirable asset to her mother's business?

Doubtful. His past was too shady. His family too sullied. He had nothing else to offer. The family was in financial shambles without full control of the Old Man's estate.

Would he do the right thing and pass it on to Zeek's mother before his death?

Zeek wouldn't put it past him to just make it so that everything was untouchable by anyone in the family. He was a spiteful old man who'd always got his way.

Until the day Zeek said no.

No more.

He drew in a deep breath of Katz' scent. Her peony perfume mingled with her personal scent—and his.

His gorilla sighed.

It was going to be tough keeping him under control. When it came to Katz, his gorilla was a single-minded domineering alpha.

Zeek had spent a lifetime keeping him in check, only letting him out to play in the fight ring, where he flourished.

He needed to find another outlet.

But for now, he was here, with her. And it was all he really needed.

He leaned forward, touching his lips to hers, lingering, gentle, sweet. "I'll take you home now," he whispered with a final brush of his mouth over hers.

15

The ballroom at the Terry estate was alive with guests, present to celebrate the engagement between Corra Terry and Darcy Karak. Ambient music, friendly conversations highlighted with laughter, and the soft clink of dishes created an atmosphere of welcome. A relaxed dinner naturally flowed into amicable mingling with digestifs and warm reunions.

Family, friends, co-workers, and classmates joined the couple for the evening of cocktails.

Corra leaned into Darcy and whispered, "I'm dying to know what your mother is discussing with my aunt."

He followed her glance toward the women in question. His sister, Katz, lingered with them, looking as though she was mediating the discussion. Zeek also stood sentinel for his mother. Darcy noted how Zeek's gaze scanned the room, always seeming to return to Katz' face.

"Probably my mother's plans to take over the world through carefully crafted business partnerships and marriage relations," he quipped and sipped from his champagne flute. "I'm sure now that she's so graciously agreed to this match, she's going to make the most of it."

Corra sighed. "Your mother looks like she's in lioness-stalking mode. Does Aunt Sheila need my guard dog interference?" she said, referring to her shifter self. She and her brother Caleb were American Staffordshire Terriers, which was why his nickname was Staff.

Darcy gave Corra's hand a light squeeze. "Despite her loving exterior, I suspect your aunt has a spine of steel and can handle herself."

"You're right. She survived our grandfather and her husband all this time." She scanned the room again. "Where is Caleb?"

"Don't worry about them tonight. This is your night. Our night to celebrate."

"He's working on your case, isn't he?"

"Your brother will be here soon. Don't worry."

Corra glanced around the room, seeking her best friend. Bryah Lam was nowhere to be seen. "Bryah is AWOL too."

"See, nothing to worry about. I'm sure they'll be here in good time."

She nodded. In the months since Bryah had found Corra's brother, Caleb, and reunited them, Corra had come to learn that Caleb was the kind of man that stood by his friends and family. He and Bryah were perfect for each other.

Corra and Bryah came from modest backgrounds. Corra was not a people-person, especially when it came to the rich and influential, like the Karak family, who were all in attendance tonight. She'd met them all before and had grown to like them. Generally, Corra didn't care what others thought of her. But she was very concerned with how her words and actions might impact Darcy or her family.

Corra deeply, deeply hated spotlights. And parties that required cocktail dresses and tuxedos.

Despite her swanky-party jitters, Corra knew that Bryah wouldn't leave her to face these people alone.

You're not alone. Not anymore.

She looked up at Darcy and laced the fingers of her free hand through his.

He smiled down at her, and her heart went wild.

Movement drew their attention to the far end of the room, where Caleb and Bryah entered the room.

Corra didn't miss Bryah's attempts to subtly adjust her dress nor Caleb's hand across the back of her shoulders as he leaned into whisper to her. She reached up and smoothed the hair on the back of her head.

Corra chuckled.

"Bryah will make a fierce agent, but she needs to work on her subtlety," Darcy murmured.

Katz must have noted their arrival. She stretched onto tiptoe to catch Darcy's attention.

Darcy squeezed Corra's hand again, tugging her toward the front of the room. "It's time."

They joined Katz, Mrs. Karak, and Aunt Sheila on a slightly raised platform, where their champagne glasses were exchanged for fresh ones.

Katz drew the guests' attention with a tiny tinkling bell and her bright smile. "Thank you all for coming this evening. I am so grateful that you traveled all this way to celebrate my brother's wonderful news." She turned her head so that she spoke to the assembled crowd. Katz seemed to freeze as her gaze met the extreme right side. Her face blanched, and she sucked in a breath, turning toward Darcy, struggling to control her expression.

Finally, she smiled at her brother.

Darcy glanced in the direction where she'd seemed to freeze and quickly stepped toward his sister, pulling Corra along with him, whispering, "Katz' future fiancé is here with his parents and friends."

On the platform, Darcy kissed Katz' cheek then his mother's and Sheila's. He turned to the assembled group, as at ease as Corra had ever seen him in any situation. She relaxed her shoulders. Little seemed to faze him.

"As Katherine said, I'm grateful you all came to share this evening with us." Hand still linked with Corra's, he pulled her hand up to his lips and kissed the backs of her fingers then grinned up at her. "I'd love for you all to meet Corra Terry, who has *willingly* agreed to marry me this summer."

Everyone chuckled.

Corra's heart pounded in her chest as she watched Darcy interact with the room full of strangers as though they were all his best friends and closest family. For all she knew, they were.

As she stood on the platform before them, her body temperature rose and her fingers shook. Darcy gave her hand a light squeeze, calming *some* of her nerves.

Most of the faces staring back at them smiled with genuine delight. There were a few that didn't.

She ignored them and focused on the faces she knew. A few were from Montreal, where she and Bryah had lived before coming to the Academy. Most were the cadets and instructors she spent her days with now. The people who were quickly becoming her chosen family.

Her gaze quickly flicked to Darcy's father and his older siblings and their spouses before landing on her best friend.

Bryah.

Her best friend. Her spirit sister.

Bryah winked at Corra, and they grinned at one another across the room.

Having finally broken free of her marathon of meetings and arrived for the night's event—fashionably late—Tonya Karak grilled her youngest daughter, Katherine, on the final details. It didn't matter that the party was in full swing.

Every function under the Karak name had to be perfect.

A shorter blonde woman, of an age with herself, smiled and approached from behind Katherine, placing a gentle hand on her shoulder to alert her of her presence.

Tonya sniffed. Controlling her instinctive urge to snarl, she forced a friendly smile onto her lips.

Sheila LeBrute. Dog shifter, like her niece and nephew, Corra and Caleb Terry.

The woman oozed kindness.

She noted the tall man who always seemed to be a step behind her. A sort of blond muscle-bound shadow.

She sniffed again. Gorilla. Her son. Troublemaker, as she recalled from her investigations into the family.

Ah, yes, I remember him now.

Katherine had said something about the young man having saved her that terrible night—the last time she'd been to this estate, when she'd had his father's throat between her lion's jaws.

Scum.

"Mrs. LeBrute." Tonya extended her hand toward the woman. "Good to be here again, under better circumstances."

"Terry. Sheila Terry," she corrected as she clasped Tonya's hand in greeting. "I've reclaimed my maiden name."

Tonya glanced to the young man who stepped forward, offering his giant hand as well.

"Zeek," he grunted.

Tonya's brow lifted as she glanced at Katherine, who turned a suspicious shade of sun-ripe peach. Tonya turned her focus back to the gorilla shifter and his mother. "Pleasure to meet you—officially. That most unpleasant evening last fall is best left forgotten. From tonight forward, once our contracts are

signed, we shall be family." Tonya beamed her most professional, assertive smile.

She'd had all this time to mourn the loss of a lucrative business partnership when she and her husband were forced to
relinquish the deal they'd spent months—years—sculpting for
Darcy.

Such a disappointment.

She stifled a sigh.

Still, he'd brought her something she could work with. A
challenge for sure. Tonya relished challenges. And this had
been a perfect one to let Katherine show her how much she'd
learned under her guidance.

Katherine wanted Darcy's vacated position on the board.

Katherine would have to earn it.

And once the final piece of the Karak matrimonial network
was locked in place, the family empire would be a legendary
force.

Tonya frowned.

It was for the best she had been overseeing Katherine's
plans, in between business take-overs and mergers. She'd
already made a gross oversight in failing to include the Aslan
family on the guest list.

Thankfully, there'd been enough time to correct that
serious social misstep.

She made a mental note to catch up with the Aslan matriarch. Tonya had been so busy that she'd not reviewed any
reports from her people on their personal and business doings.

Sheila Terry was speaking again. "...so grateful to work with
Katz on our new business plan. I'm confident her consultation
will result in a strong launch of our new business services. She's a
very knowledgeable young woman. You must be so proud of her."

"Mmm, yes, we're very proud of her accomplishments, as
we are of all of our children," Tonya said. Her gaze swept the

room then fell to her diamond studded watch. "Katherine. It's time."

"We're waiting on two more key guests," Katherine said, scanning the room herself. After a moment, she added, "Ah, there they are. They've just stepped in."

She stood on tiptoe, catching Darcy's attention. Darcy and Corra made their way toward the platform.

Tonya smiled at her youngest son as he leaned in to kiss his fiancée's cheek. She stood aside to let the younger people have their shining moment. Her eyes caught her beloved husband's, standing amid their older children. Derek winked and raised his champagne flute to her in salute. Despite the smudges of salt and pepper at his temples and a few extra laugh lines, Derek looked the same as he did on the day he swept her off her feet. She tossed a length of hair over her shoulder and gave him a coy smile in return before bringing her attention back to the proceedings.

They made their pronouncements, and everyone raised their glasses to officiate the moment.

There was no going back now.

Everyone cheered and drank and clapped. The mingling resumed.

"Come along, Katherine," Tonya said, drawing her youngest daughter from the conversation she'd been about to engage in with the Terry family. "It's time to go and speak with the Aslans. They've waited long enough, and now that Darcy is set, we will finalize the details for you."

"The Aslans? Karen & Jason Aslan?" Sheila Terry asked.

"Yes. You're aware of them?" Tonya smiled.

A frown wrinkled Sheila's brow as she glanced at her son's impassive face. "Yes, I am," she said carefully.

"New business partners?" Corra asked, sipping her drink.

Tonya studied her future daughter-in-law before answering. "Yes, indeed. As well as Katherine's future in-laws. She's to marry their son, Trent. And now that Darcy is settled so quickly, we can move up the timeline on this agreement, too."

The tall, blond gorilla shifter stepped closer to Katharine's back, stance rigid.

"Mother, now isn't the time for this. It's Darcy and Corra's night to celebrate. There's no need to rush."

Tonya glanced from her daughter's flushed face up to the man behind her.

Oh, yes there is.

She smiled. "This is the best time to set up meetings to finalize things. Remember what I taught you, Katharine. Every social meeting is a networking opportunity. Come along." She turned and took three steps before she heard an exclamation behind her and whirled around to see what had happened.

Fuck.

"Come along, Katherine," Katz' mother said, cutting into the congratulations she offered to her brother Darcy and future sister-in-law, Corra.

As her mother spoke, ice swept Katz' body. She'd seen Trent and his parents at the center of the room and nearly panicked and let loose a string of curses, realizing Mother had caught her omission and must have sent an invitation herself.

Katz's lips tightened on another round of inappropriate words as her mother and Sheila talked.

Katz felt Zeek step closer to her.

Heat radiated between them, causing her heart to pound. "Mother, now isn't the time for this. It's Darcy and Corra's night to celebrate. There's no need to rush."

Mother glanced from Katz' flushed face up to Zeek's behind her; her expression was enough to signal the trouble coming.

Mother widened her smile, baring her white teeth. "This is

the best time to set up meetings to finalize things. Remember what I taught you, Katharine. Every social meeting is a networking opportunity. Come along." She turned her back on Katz, expecting her to follow.

Determined not to look at anyone before following her mother, Katz moved to step down from the platform they all still occupied.

Strong hands spun her around.

Wide-eyed, she blinked up into Zeek's scowling face before his lips descended to claim hers.

"Oh, my!" someone beside her said. Sheila maybe? She couldn't be sure.

That was all she registered before she gave in to the sensation of Zeek's demanding lips and crushing arms. Her own encircled his waist without her permission as she sank into him.

Zeek's gorilla beat his chest as he absorbed the conversation between Katz and her mother.

Fiancé.

Katz' *future* fiancé was here. Now.

Instinct overwhelmed his civilized brain. He grasped Katz' arms before she followed her mother to this faceless rival.

His lips claimed hers.

Mine. My kitty. No one else's. Ever.

She already knew it.

Now, everyone else would too.

His gorilla growled in triumph when Katz' arms encircled his waist, her entire body molding to his. A soft rumble against his chest made him smile.

His kitty purred for him.

He ended the kiss with a soft nibble on her full lips.

The silence of the room slowly registered. He opened his eyes at the room of onlookers.

His gaze slid to Mrs. Karak's frosty glare.

He smirked, and her ice instantly turned to fire.

"We're in so much doo-doo," Katz whispered, without daring to look at anyone other than Zeek in that moment.

With that display, Mrs. Karak couldn't exactly resume her pointed trek to reunite Katz with—what was his name?—Trent and his family.

He gulped but held his ground.

If Katz wouldn't stand up for herself, he would do it for her.

"It's worth it. You're worth it, Katz." He brushed his lips across hers and released her.

16

I can't breathe.

Katz was crushed to Zeek's chest, his warm lips against hers, his scent embedded into her brain.

And she didn't want to move.

Just feel.

Feel *all* of him.

Her heart pounded so hard in her chest it ached.

Everything about this moment was perfect.

Except the faraway recollection that they weren't alone.

She was calm, grounded by his embrace, yet floating from his presence.

Simple.

Honest.

True.

Zeek released her lips. Air rushed back into her lungs, bringing clarity with it.

Oh no!

What did we just do?

They'd usurped Darcy and Corra's moment.

Their mother's moment.

Oh sweet Isis.

Katz blinked. Zeek's face filled her vision.

His lips, the strong jaw, straight nose.

Her eyes lifted to his. They glittered as they stared back at her from beneath his thick brows.

The intensity of his soulful gaze threatened to steal her breath away again. Make her unable to think anymore.

I don't want to think anymore.

But she did think. And it ruined the moment.

Her attention slid from Zeek, who occupied her entire field of vision, to their surroundings.

Sound. The low ambient music. A few whispers, but otherwise, silence. She knew if she looked, everyone would be looking at them.

"Don't look at them," Zeek whispered as though he knew exactly what she'd been thinking.

"What have we done?" she whispered back. She swallowed.

"Made a statement." His eyes twinkled, and a slow grin changed his expression.

Her breath hitched on his sexiness.

She licked her dry lips. "But I didn't…"

"Sure, you did."

Yes. I did.

"Now what?"

He leaned closer, lips brushing her ear.

She shivered.

"Whatever the fuck *we* want, kitten."

"But my mother—"

"Can't do a thing about it."

"Oh, Zeek," she said. The rush of sadness filled those two words. Tears blinded her. "You have no idea."

He straightened, looking down into her face. "Don't I?"

No. He was right. He did. She'd met his grandfather. And father.

"Okay."

Suddenly, she heard furious whispering from somewhere behind her and foot stomps toward them.

As she turned toward whoever was approaching, she was jerked backwards by a hard grip on her arm.

Oh shit.

She stumbled backwards.

"That's my fiancée," Trent Aslan growled in Zeek's face, almost nose to nose.

Katz looked around the room. Everyone indeed was staring.

Her mother glared, rooted to her place next to Trent's parents, who'd moved to join her.

This is bad.

"Is she?" Zeek smirked.

Trent jerked his head. "Since childhood."

"Zeek, not now," Caleb growled at his cousin.

Zeek didn't look at Caleb. He turned his gaze to Katz, who drew his attention to Corra instead.

He straightened and brushed past Trent, who stood in his space, to approach Corra.

"Congratulations to you both." He bent to kiss Corra's cheek and dropped his voice, but Katz was still close enough to hear. "I'm sorry to disrupt your night, cousin."

"Don't be," she said, returning the kiss to his cheek. "Just figure it out."

She smiled up at him then at Katz with a wink.

Katz watched all of this, heart hammering. When he looked back in her direction again, she took a step forward—toward him—but the slight shake of his head stayed her.

He walked toward his mother, kissed her cheek, gave Katz' mother a brief nod, then left the room.

Conversation resumed.

"What was that all about?"

"That was spicy!"

"Brute. She's clearly engaged to that other guy!"

"A love triangle—how romantic!"

"This family is a cesspool of unending drama."

And on it went.

Trent turned on her. "Can you believe that guy?"

She studied him for a moment then dropped her voice so only he would hear. "Don't ever touch me like that again."

"What? He was mauling you."

She lifted a brow, shrugging her bare arm forward, where the only blemishes on her near-flawless skin were the angry imprints of his fingers.

He avoided her pointed stare but didn't apologize.

"The contract is all but signed and initialed. I won't have other men interfering with what's mine."

Katz scoffed. "When did you develop an interest in me or anything I do? We haven't seen each other in years, and *now* you're suddenly invested?"

"Your brother is settled. We're next. I won't have you embarrassing my family. They waited too long for this."

As has mine. Too much is on the line.

The weight of expectation squeezed in on her.

Is this how her older siblings felt before their marriages?

She glanced toward her brothers and sister. She knew how much effort their father had put into making their matches. They all seemed happy enough.

"You've changed since you went away to college."

"Yeah? So? Doesn't everyone?"

"Maybe." She glanced toward his friends. One, the weasel, eyed her with a sly expression. That one was familiar. Where had she seen him before? The woodpecker shifter, on the other hand, looked as though he were just waiting for Trent to break the contract so he could get a taste of her himself.

She shuddered. Both were revolting. "Interesting company you keep."

"They're good guys. Been friends forever."

"Since college?"

"Yeah."

"Huh," she said.

"What?"

"Oh, nothing. Just…interesting."

The weasel… Yes! He was with that group at the restaurant and then the fight club. Did Trent know what kind of company his *buddy* kept?

I'm going to have a chat with Mummy and Daddy.

Shit.

I've just royally fucked things up for Katz.

Zeek paced the hallway.

Man, I want a smoke.

But he'd given that up ages ago and was glad for it.

Still.

While his stomach roiled with guilt over causing problems for her with her parents, his heart fluttered, *knowing*. Knowing that she wanted him. She would have left the party with him, if he hadn't indicated she should stay.

"But, sir, I must insist that you produce an invitation before I grant your admittance." Mr. Charbonneau, the butler's, raised voice was distinct as it carried down the hallway.

Zeek strode toward the front door.

Fuck.

Garcia.

"What the hell are you doing here?" he demanded, heart pounding.

"Just here to offer my congratulations."

"With armed guards?" He looked pointedly at the goons flanking him.

Zeek's mind raced.

Fuck, fuck, fuck.

Were Caleb's and Darcy's covers blown?

A large contingent of party guests were FUC agents and cadets.

"Don't mind them. They're just my shadows."

"Well, your armed shadows will have to stay outside the house."

Garcia signaled for his men to stay behind.

Zeek moved aside to grant him entrance. "Please announce Mr. Garcia's presence," he said to Charbonneau, who gave a short bow and disappeared down the hall toward the party.

"There are rumors you're returning to the ring after a long vacation," Garcia said.

"I didn't think you listened to gossip."

"Only when it interests me." He eyed Zeek with a sly grin. "On that note, I have to admit I was intrigued to learn of the connection between your family and the Karak family. Very intrigued. You'll introduce me of course. Publicly, I mean. I've already met two of the Karak cubs. I'm interested in the matriarch. We could do business."

Not fucking likely, if I can help it.

But as it turned out, he couldn't help it.

As he opened his mouth to deflect the issue, Katz, Darcy, and their mother emerged from the ballroom.

"I will have to spend a significant amount of my time smoothing this over and likely giving up concessions on this contract I was not prepared to make in order to secure this business alliance. Their connections through their marketing company are a valuable asset. It's bad enough I had to give up an entire corporation for your brother. I'm not going to lose on this matter too. Your father is doing his best to lower their hackles after that little display." Mrs. Karak's hard voice carried down the finely polished corridor toward Zeek and the new guest.

The butler cleared his throat to politely indicate the family was not alone in the hall.

"Sounds like I missed a bit of theatrics," Garcia said wryly.

Mrs. Karak spun on her heel. Her expression quickly slipped from ferocious scowl through surprise to settle on a thin mask of social approachability.

Katz and Darcy exchanged glances when they saw who Zeek was speaking to.

Garcia prowled down the hall to meet the trio. "The famous Mrs. Karak. I simply could not miss out on the opportunity to meet such a fearless businesswoman."

Her smile was cool, but curious. "You have me at a disadvantage, Mr…"

"Phil Garcia. Sports and gaming investor," he said, taking her slim fingers in his.

Zeek couldn't tell if she was truly ignorant of his identity or not. She gave no indication. She maintained a perfectly polite expression.

Remind me never to play poker with this woman.

Garcia then turned to Katz and Darcy. "Wonderful to see you again so soon. I've come to congratulate you on your engagement to Ms. Terry. You should have told me of your connections," he admonished them good-naturedly.

Katz gave a light laugh. "Such a small world, isn't it?"

Zeek detected the strained note in her voice. "I'll find my mother so you can speak with her and be on your way."

"Oh, no need to hurry." To the butler, Garcia said, "I'll have a drink while I wait."

Mr. Charbonneau stiffened almost imperceptibly but nodded and left to do as asked.

"Tell me more about what you do and how you met my youngest children, Mr. Garcia," Mrs. Karak said.

Zeek was torn between trying to keep Garcia away from Mrs. Karak, whom he was sure wouldn't see the connection as an advantage, and trying to keep him away from the rest of the guests.

He didn't want this man anywhere near his mother after the problems he'd already been stirring up, but at this point, he wasn't sure there was a choice. Any which way was problematic.

He decided to take his cue from Mrs. Karak's engagement in the hall and darted into the ballroom to extract his mother. Corra and Caleb came with her, and they all moved into the study. The one that had been his grandfather's and had been transformed into Sheila's domain.

17

Katz swallowed the acid gathering in her throat, desperate to avoid puking as she stared between Garcia and her mother in Sheila's newly renovated study.

Everything was going to shit tonight. After all the hard work she and Sheila had put into planning this evening to make it perfect for Darcy and Corra, it was all going to shit.

One thing after another. And when she thought things couldn't get worse... surprise!

Whatever was about to happen, it was clear they needed to keep this man out of the ballroom. His presence would severely jeopardize everyone's social standing—if he were recognized.

But hadn't she already done that? When she'd interfered with Darcy's surveillance and gotten them into the fight club?

Her mother was going to tear them apart with her teeth once the evening was over.

Katz laughed, drawing everyone's attention as soon as Mr. Charbonneau made his rounds with a tray of drinks.

"It's incredible, really. Serendipitous." She waved her glass of champagne. She turned to her mother. "Darcy and I went out for dinner to celebrate his coming engagement—just the two of us—when we ran into Mr. Harper at the restaurant, entertaining a group of friends." She tapped a finger to her lips and looked at Darcy. "As I recall, one of his guests is here tonight with Trent. Anyway, I digress. Mr. Harper insisted Darcy and I attend an event with him. You know, a little 'manly man' entertainment before getting hitched kind of event."

Her mother lifted a brow. Her lips thinned.

Darcy cut in. "It was quite a surprise, and neither of us wanted to be rude to a long-time business friend of yours, Mother. So we agreed to go." Darcy gave the same short laugh Katz had. "Turned out to be a fight ring. Imagine that? And Mr. Harper introduced us to Mr. Garcia here. I do apologize, Mr. Garcia. Neither of us had had the time to pass along your request to meet my mother, but it seems the situation has remedied itself."

Garcia cut in. "It's curious you didn't give any indication that you knew Zeek and Caleb when they arrived at my club."

She gulped, eyes darting between Zeek and Darcy.

Dear Isis. I can't screw up Darcy's case. He and Caleb have been working too hard on this.

"She wouldn't, Mr. Garcia. There has been some… miscommunication between our two families." Mother unexpectedly stepped in to smooth over whatever was happening here. "Just a private little inter-family spat that's been resolved—in time for the engagement party."

Sheila finally cut in. "Mr. Garcia, thank you for coming all the way out here to pay your respects to my niece and her fiancé, but the party will be breaking up soon and the guests heading out. You may want to beat the rush. We can arrange a business meeting later in the week to discuss what's on your mind when everyone is fresh."

"Tomorrow. You may come to my office. I will expect you at ten a.m., when we can discuss your father's business and the family's intentions moving forward. You've had plenty of time to consider my... offers." He turned to Katz' mother. "Now that we've been properly introduced, I will reach out to set up a lunch with you as well, madame." He bent over her hand again and made his exit without looking at anyone else.

The door clicked shut, and the sound of his heels disappeared down the hall.

"What the hell was that?" Katz' mother demanded.

Zeek strode to the door and locked it.

Katz swallowed, staring into her mother's furious face. She hadn't seen her this incensed since... since Corra walked out on her last fall during a family dinner.

"That is the kind of man my mother has been trying to break away from and that Katz has been helping her to build her own legitimate business to avoid," Zeek said to Mrs. Karak.

Darcy blew out a breath. Some obscure mental exchange happened between him and Caleb, who gave him a nod. To Mrs. Karak, Darcy said, "Garcia is the target of our case."

"You're working to bring that man down?" Mother said, incredulous.

"He's an underground fight club gangster," Caleb said, "like my grandfather was before his arrest. Darcy and I have been working to bring him to justice with the Council, but it's been difficult finding the right kind of evidence."

Katz' mother pulled a face. "They're illegal in the human world if the fighters make money from it. But that's not necessarily true for shifters—depending on the district."

Darcy nodded. "Right. And in this case, Garcia has a history of extortion and outright force."

"It's common knowledge but counted as rumor. None of it has been solidly substantiated," Caleb added.

"We're working to find shifters willing to testify, but nobody is."

"They're all too scared," Sheila added, nodding. "It was the same with my father. No one crosses someone like that."

"Except you?" Mrs. Karak said to Sheila.

Sheila's smile was grim. "Yes. I have denied his demands."

"Which were?"

"He wants a union of sorts. An acknowledgment of his sole power in this region, in the fight world."

Mrs. Karak nodded. "Collaboration or endorsement. What would he want with me?"

Sheila shrugged. "Who knows. But we should be getting back to our guests now that he's gone. They'll be wondering where the star couple is."

Caleb laughed. "They'll just think they snuck away to consummate their vows way early."

Corra shoved her brother's shoulder and grumbled, "You're one to talk."

Zeek watched the interaction between the siblings. A pang of loneliness struck him. He was happy that they'd been reunited. Happy to have a new cousin in Corra. But for a long time, he and Caleb had been like brothers. Until their paths diverged and became strained.

But things were changing. Zeek was working hard to do better.

Deep down, he hoped that maybe, just maybe, he could mend the rift between them and they could be family again.

Maybe.

Still standing by the door, he moved to open it for Corra as she and Darcy approached on their return to the party. She looked up at him with a smile that warmed his heart.

Despite recent events, she seemed to have forgiven him.

He hoped Caleb would too.

Caleb followed Darcy out into the hall where they had a murmured exchange.

Bryah stopped before Zeek and grinned. "Hey, King Kong Junior, you should grab your girl and climb the highest tower. I recommend one that her lioness mother can't follow. Try the roof—it has a great view," she whispered with a wink and slipped out of the room.

Zeek chuckled, glancing up at Katz, who stood with her mother in a heated exchange.

Both scowled at one another. "It was the deal, Katherine. You agreed."

"But—"

"No objections. A deal is a deal. Now I have to go and spend the rest of the evening pulling the tattered pieces of this contract back together and smooth the raised hackles thanks to your little display in there."

"Can you just listen—"

"I've heard—and seen—enough." To Sheila, Mrs. Karak said, "Garcia is expecting a business meeting with you in the morning, and me sometime soon. I propose we go together and you fill me in on everything you know about this man and what nonsense my son has gotten himself into with this FUC'n case."

Sheila stiffened. "The work he and Caleb are doing is important. Caleb's whole purpose in becoming a FUC agent was to bring down bad guys like Garcia and end the tyranny they reap."

"Like your father?" Mrs. Karak said, brow raised.

"Yes," Sheila growled. "Exactly like my father."

Zeek stepped closer to his mother. He'd only ever heard her growl when the topic of his own father, Rollo, was brought up.

Mrs. Karak sniffed, assessing Zeek and his mother before she spun on her heel. "Katherine. Party."

Katz' skin flushed. Her eyes glittered as she glared at her

mother, but she fell in line and returned to the engagement party.

Zeek glanced down at his mother when he felt her gentle touch on his arm. He patted her hand, and she lay her head on his shoulder.

"What do you want to do about Garcia?"

She sighed. "That was a bold move coming here tonight."

"I'll support you if you want to take over the Old Man's position."

"No, Zeek. That era has to end. Caleb is right to do this within shifter council law. You and I know what these displays mean because we know the language. But they don't *prove* anything in a council court. He pushes the line but hasn't crossed it. That's how my father operated too. When the line *is* crossed, no one is willing to corroborate it."

"Do you think he has any idea Caleb is working for FUC now?"

"I don't know. I hope not. It's dangerous, and I don't know if he and Darcy can handle this."

"They'd have other FUC agents involved when the time comes."

"I don't know... Our relationship with the agency hasn't been... cozy, thanks to my father. I just worry about those two boys, that they're getting in over their head. You know that better than anyone."

Yes. He did.

And now more and more people he cared about were slipping deeper into the mire of his world.

His old world.

He looked down into his mother's kind face.

He'd never asked himself what his involvement in that world might have meant for her. At the time, he'd only thought of following his father's orders to please his grandfather. That, one day, he might take their place. He'd hoped that, one day, all that bullshit would be worth it. That he and Caleb, together, would lead the family into the next generation.

Do things differently.

But in order to do things differently in the future, he had to go back to his old world now.

Be that old Zeek.

And hope that, after that, he could leave that old Zeek behind once and for all.

If— If he wasn't swallowed up by it.

18

Katz lingered outside the study, waiting for Zeek to emerge. Muffled music drifted through the house. Her mother had returned to the guests to try to mend the tear that her and Zeek's public kiss had caused with the Aslans.

Zeek's expression registered surprise when he stepped into the hall, his mother a few steps behind.

Sheila smiled at Katz and brushed her arm with a light touch before returning to the party, leaving them alone.

Zeek dipped his head, looking up at her from beneath his thick brows, scratching at one with his thumb. "I, uh, I'm sorry about that public display in there. I just—"

"Don't be," she cut in, stepping closer to him, looking up into his bashful face. "I'm not."

"But it doesn't change anything."

Her heart twisted.

"I know my mother. She won't let this go. She gave up one valuable deal for Darcy, and she's been waiting even longer for this one."

Zeek snorted and stepped back. "Our family isn't good enough."

"Your family doesn't meet her business needs. It's not the same." She reached for him.

He caught her hand in his. He kissed her palm and said, "It feels the same."

She shivered at his touch and the huskiness of his voice.

"This is why I stayed away. Why I tried to push you away." She blinked through tears. "Because I knew this would happen and I'd feel this way and that you might too. All those stolen nights we had when nobody cared what I did was paradise, Zeek. It was everything that I ever wanted. Just you and me. No one else. No obligations." She swallowed. "But outside of that room, we were both bound to our families. So it couldn't last. We both knew it."

He nodded, said nothing.

He looked deep into her eyes, nostrils flaring as he scented her, as his hands cupped her face, exactly as he'd done that very first night outside The Hub.

She shivered, leaning into his warm body.

His head descended. His lips brushed hers once, twice, and on the third, she opened to taste him. His tongue swiped hers, and she moaned.

He didn't release her face but held her fast. Her hands roamed his body, her fingers and palms memorizing the feel of him.

She wanted to feel the crush of his arms, the steeliness of his body inside of hers, the beat of his heart beneath her ear.

She got none of it.

He released her mouth with a sigh, pressing his forehead to hers.

"I love you, kitten," he whispered, releasing her face. He turned his back on her and strode down the hall without looking back.

Katz stared after him, rooted in place. Her lips tingled, her heart pounded, her gut twisted. But her feet wouldn't move.

I love you, kitten.

He disappeared around a corner, and the spell broke, releasing the tension from her body.

I love you too, Zeek.

Drawing a shuddering breath, she straightened, checked herself over, and moved toward a mirror suspended at the end of the hall to ensure she was still presentable. A disheveled, heart-sore kitten stared back at her. Tucking her hair back into place and righting her dress, she schooled her features into the coolest socialite mask she could muster.

Katz straightened her spine then strode back to the party to celebrate her brother's happiness.

Zeek went to his old room at the far end of the mansion. He grabbed a bag from the back of the closet and filled it with clothes he'd left here.

He wouldn't be going back to the Academy.

He knew what he had to do.

Zeek needed to go and fight for Garcia. That was what Garcia really wanted.

Fighting for Garcia would get the man off his mother's tail and give her breathing space to get her business up and flourishing.

Fighting for Garcia would also humiliate his grandfather, which was what Garcia wanted more than anything else.

The rivalry between Garcia and Old Man Terry was old and deep. They'd been friends once. Partners. One had betrayed the other. Zeek didn't know the details but had picked up the gist of it over the years.

Once, and only once, in a small fit of rebellion against his father and grandfather, Zeek had gone to Garcia and offered to fight for him and had done so until his grandfather's rage brought him back. And his father's *lessons* ensured it didn't happen again.

It was the only time he'd ever tried to leave.

So, yeah, when Caleb left for the Academy without as much fuss, Zeek had been bitterly jealous. But then, Caleb hadn't been stupid and gone to the enemy.

This time when he went to the enemy, it was to end it all.

Leaving his room, he paused in the hall, listening to the distant music celebrating his cousin Corra's engagement to Darcy Karak, the son of a powerful business mogul.

Both Zeek and Katz had given up a lot to give them the chance to be happy. And they were both determined to ensure it would continue.

If Katz could do what was needed for the family she loved so much, so could Zeek.

19

Katz picked at her breakfast.

Zeek hadn't returned to the party.

All she could think about was that last kiss, an echo of their first kiss.

"Katherine." Her mother's crisp voice pulled her from her thoughts.

She sighed and picked up her coffee cup. "Mother." She sipped her brew as acid rode her esophagus.

"You'll be pleased to know I've nearly smoothed things over with the Aslans. We're back on track. I just had to make some more concessions to accommodate your…indiscretions."

Katz slammed her mug back onto the table. "Indiscretions?"

Her mother lifted a brow at the childish outburst. "Yes, indiscretions. That little display cost us. A lot. But thankfully, not everything."

"Why is this so important to you? Have you ever, just once, stopped to think through every one of your children's matches and paused to consider that maybe some of us, if not all, had no desire to do this?"

"You never protested before, Katherine. Interesting you

have objections now that it's your turn." Mrs. Karak sniffed at the food placed before her and pushed the plate away.

Katz swallowed. She couldn't argue that. She'd been so wrapped up in doing all she could, to be the very best shadow of her mother that she could be, that she hadn't thought on it over much. Not until Darcy cracked the lid on their mother's carefully sealed recipe of family business procedure.

Her mother went on. "I'm determined to turn this situation with Darcy around to our own benefit. I have little desire to enter into any kind of a business deal with that Garcia person, but I am curious as to what he thinks he can bring to our table. As a pure thug, I doubt it's much. But I'm curious enough to give him an hour of my time."

Katz didn't answer.

"We'll be in the city anyway. You and I are meeting with the Aslans, who returned there last night. We have a lunch before they fly out."

Katz glared at her mother.

"Good morning!" Sheila's cheery voice cut the building tension between Katz and her mother.

Katz turned her attention to Sheila and offered her a bright smile. "Good morning."

"Your party was a resounding success, Katz. Everyone had nothing but praise for your efforts as they left last night."

Mrs. Karak sniffed.

Katz ignored her. "I'm glad it all went well."

"All things considered," Mother cut in.

"Party crashers are to be expected."

"I'm referring to your son publicly claiming my daughter in front of her future fiancé and his family."

Sheila stiffened. Her lips thinned as she regarded Katz' mother. "My son clearly has feelings for your daughter," she said carefully then slid her astute gaze to Katz, waiting for her to add more.

Katz cleared her throat and dropped her gaze from Sheila's. "It doesn't matter." She flicked her gaze back up to Sheila again. "I made a promise to the Aslans and my mother that I have to keep."

"What kind of promise is worth giving up someone who loves you?"

Katz dry-swallowed the lump in her throat.

"Family duty."

Sheila's laugh was short and bitter. "Family duty. I know a lot about that. I made a lot of mistakes trying to toe that particular line."

"I'm not like you. And neither is my daughter." Mrs. Karak's voice sliced through the room.

"No." Sheila's voice, just as sharp, brooked no chance of dismissal. "You are dragging your family down a road dangerously similar to the one my father forced us to take. Be careful, Mrs. Karak. Be very careful. Enjoy your breakfast. I have several things to do before we leave to meet Garcia."

Katz' eyes followed Sheila as she rose from the table and left the room.

She felt her mother's stare when she reclaimed her coffee cup. "Yes, Mother, I love him. No, I don't want to marry Trent Aslan or take over his parents' company for you. But I will do it, as I said, for Darcy."

"I don't care who you do it for, as long as you do it." Her mother left the room.

Katz sucked in a deep breath the second her mother passed the threshold.

She reminded herself that she loved her mother.

She meant well.

Most of the time.

Zeek called Caleb's cell.

"Yeah?"

"I'm in the city, and I need your help."

There was a long silence on the line. "I wondered where you went last night. I thought you were done with all of this, Zeek. Which district jail do I need to bail you out of?"

Zeek kept his voice low. "It's not what you think, Caleb. And I'm in the jail closest to Garcia's club. As my fight manager, you need to be seen getting me out, or this won't work."

"Shit, Zeek, you should have talked to me first, man. If things go sideways—"

"They won't. Get me out."

"Coming."

The call disconnected. Now Zeek just had to wait. He had a lot to tell Caleb already.

20

Sheila's SUV held the silence of a hollowed-out iceberg.

Katz shared the backseat with her mother, where the temperature was even more frigid.

Normally, when Mrs. Karak was in one of these moods, Katz would either try to ease it or act as though nothing was wrong.

This time she did neither.

Sheila was also quietly thoughtful, riding up front next to her driver until they reached the address Garcia had emailed to Sheila.

Katz recognized it immediately.

Now, she sat in the waiting room of his office suites, positioned in the opposite side of the same city block where the fight club had been.

Sheila was in one board room, her mother in another.

Through the frosted glass wall, Sheila's shadow paced the length of the room. There was no movement behind her mother's glass wall.

There wouldn't be.

"Ah, Ms. Karak. Good morning." Garcia's pleasant tone

drew her attention away from the boardrooms. He stood, smiling at her, his gaze intent.

She tried to hide the shudder that racked her body under his leering attention. She stood, offered her hand and a polite nod. "Mr. Garcia."

"I have heard a lot about you these last couple of days." His eyes slid up and down her body.

"Oh?" She covered her alarm with mild curiosity and a friendly smile. "Good things, I hope."

"Yes. Very good things." He broke off his inspection, swinging his attention toward the two boardrooms. "Business first. Pleasure later." He smiled and moved toward Sheila's room first.

Katz was too unnerved to reclaim her seat.

What did he want from them? From her? The way his gaze slid all over her it had left little doubt that he appreciated her physically, but she had the underlying suspicion there was something else he wanted from her, even though he was meeting with Sheila and her mother.

A chunk of that iceberg broke off and slid down her spine, settling somewhere in the bottom of her gut.

She rubbed her palms together, trying to ground herself and refrain from pacing.

Her fingers itched to text Zeek. To talk to him. To see him.

Instead, she shoved her hands into her pants pockets and stared at a generic painting above the guest sofa. To calm her nerves over the meetings, she turned her thoughts to Zeek and that kiss last night.

She'd been prepared to leave the party with him.

That kiss—his declaration was clear. As was his acknowledgment of her claimed obligations.

Her heart swelled. He wanted her. As much as she wanted him.

A life with him. Open and carefree. Not secret and hidden to hotel rooms and the back of his truck.

She glanced toward the door that blocked her view from her mother.

Corra had won Mrs. Karak's respect. But Katz had also leveraged her acceptance of the match.

A promise to adhere to the proposal to marry Trent Aslan and do everything she could to raise the Terry family's social and financial standing to her mother's standards when the engagement went public. The party was a start.

She'd always been indifferent to Trent Aslan. He was something down the road in the long-distant future. She hadn't expected to catch up to the future so damned fast. Nor had she expected to fall in love with someone like Zeek.

Her big-hearted gorilla with soulful eyes.

Just thinking about him made her heart pound and body tingle.

There was nothing about Trent Aslan that made any part of her pound or tingle. He was as bland as the painting she faced with such disinterest.

She sighed and dropped to the sofa, giving up on even trying to feign interest in the painting.

Is that what her marriage to Trent would be like? Bland?

Apathetic?

The thought of letting him touch her brought as much disdain as the idea of Garcia's sudden interest.

Well, if that remained the case, then her mother and father were going to be seriously disappointed on the grandchildren front. This marriage her mother wanted so badly might bring her the united social and financial power she wanted.

But it wouldn't last if there were no heirs.

Katz relaxed against the back of the sofa as she followed this new train of thought while she waited.

"We're only going to have one shot at this. Garcia is smarter than he looks," Zeek said to Caleb as soon as they were in his truck.

"You're doing the right thing, Zeek. Thanks, man."

Zeek nodded. He felt it in his gut. Caleb was right. Always had been.

Zeek just hadn't been in the right head space to accept it and do anything about it.

Things were different now.

I'm different.

All Caleb had ever wanted was to stop these fight rings that forced fighters to participate. There were some that fought because they wanted to but not all. And those were the ones that Caleb was focused on.

Caleb called Joe Suricatta from his cell and put him on speaker. "Zeek has some news for us."

"Go on," Joe said.

"There's a fight coming up. I spent the night catching up with old fight buddies at the bar last night and meeting new guys in the scene."

"And?"

"Guys talk, but they're careful. You have to know how to read between the lines. Some are tired and talk about retiring but can't. Some of the new guys are hyped and determined to make a name for themselves before moving into the regulated professional world but are hesitant. And there were hints about some special fighters that are only ever seen in the ring on special nights. And this particular fight is one of those nights."

"Why this one?" Caleb asked.

Zeek shrugged. "Garcia has a special guest."

"Caleb, what is your plan?"

Zeek spoke before Caleb could open his mouth. "I'm set to

fight tonight. Caleb will be my manager. We can probably get Darcy into Garcia's circle."

"Do it. I'll inform Miranda and Chase. If we can get what we need to move in, we'll be ready."

"The timing has to be right. Garcia is dangerous."

"Understood," Joe said, then ended the call.

"Are you sure you want to do this, Zeek?" Caleb studied his cousin's face.

"Yeah. It's time I fight for the right reasons. Like you do."

"If we bring him down, that will be it. I won't ask anything else of you."

Zeek gave a short laugh. "*When* we bring him down. Who knows, maybe I'll catch the agent bug and enroll as a cadet myself after I finish out my term as an instructor."

"Whatever you decide to do, you'll be an asset to the organization." Caleb grinned.

21

Acid churned in Katz' gut as she followed her mother to their luncheon with the Aslans.

Sheila had left Garcia's boardroom ashen, though she tried to mask her distress when she said her good-byes to Katz and left the building.

Katz' mother had emerged from her meeting with Garcia wearing a flinty expression that marked trouble.

Both women were tight-lipped about their exchange with the gangster.

Mother opted to walk the four city blocks from Garcia's offices to the restaurant. She set an impressive pace, considering the pumps she wore.

Clearly, she was burning through a plan.

Katz kept up, mindful not to turn an ankle or drag a heel.

Sweet Isis, how much worse could things get?

The restaurant hostess led them straight to the Aslans' table.

"Karen, Jason," Mother said, without leaning to kiss their cheeks when they stood to greet her.

The couple exchanged glances, their warm expressions cooling.

"We've already ordered coffee. What would you like?" Jason said as she and Katz took their seats.

Karen gave Katz a curt nod.

Whatever Mother had talked them into, clearly neither was pleased to see Katz.

"Nothing. This meeting won't be long. The contract we were working on is no longer viable."

Katz' heart hit the bottom of her stomach and bounced back up into her throat. "What? Why?"

"But you said just yesterday how important this partnership was to you," Karen sputtered. Jason gaped at Mrs. Karak.

"That was yesterday."

Katz was giddy with euphoria and terror.

The engagement to Trent was off.

Why? What happened?

Oh no. Garcia.

Oh, sweet Isis, no.

She gulped, eyes glued to her mother. It was difficult to hear over her pulse whooshing through her head. Palms slick, she stared from Jason to Karen, who stared at her mother, pale.

Her mother, however, waved a hand. "Our interests no longer align."

"You can't just—"

"I can and will. Your son owes an awful lot of money in gambling debts across the country and in illegal fight rings. His companions are also leaving marks of their own. One has a coast-to-coast string of impregnated dancers looking for support, and the other is engaging in blackmail and embezzlement."

Karen blanched. Jason's mouth snapped shut.

She went on, "But I think you knew that already." Her fingers drummed on the tabletop.

"You've been waiting a decade for this deal. And you're just going to drop us?"

Katz' gaze bounced between Karen and her mother.

"Yesterday, you insulted my family's integrity and commitment toward a stronger partnership. You insulted us, while your son has been circling the bowl for years." Her gaze flicked from Karen to Jason. Her lips twisted with distaste. "Sometimes, you let the lame gazelle you've been stalking for days limp its way back to the herd of the *ordinary* when a fatter prey wanders into your path." She shrugged.

Karen snapped upright, indignant. "We are *not* lame gazelles, Tonya."

Mother smirked and rose from her seat. "We're done here. Move on. I have."

Silent, Katz followed suit.

Karen glared at Katz' mother. Jason slumped in his chair, dejected.

They'd just lost everything.

This meeting had been set up to sign the agreement.

Her mother had just destroyed them with her rejection, both socially and financially.

The fist clenching her heart released, and she breathed a sigh of relief. She didn't have to marry Trent, now or ever.

Her gaze shot to her mother's back as she followed her out of the door. Katz was still a piece in her mother's game. The only problem now was that she had no idea on which board they were playing.

At least the Aslans were a known factor.

Her thoughts returned to the meeting they'd just left with Garcia. The fist returned to grip even tighter as she reconsidered her earlier suspicion that her mother would make a deal with him.

Her mother strode along the sidewalk with a lighter step.

She wouldn't really… would she?

What else had Garcia said to her?

"Where are we going?" Katz asked her mother.

"Shopping! I feel like celebrating."

"Shopping?" Katz stumbled as her heel dragged across a crack in the sidewalk.

Is she insane?

"Celebrate what?" Katz gaped, semi-hoping as she tried to adjust her shoe and keep up with her mother.

"A new venture."

"Mother! What new venture? What are you talking about? Can we stop and talk about what just happened?"

Her mother paused, looking back at Katz with a gleam in her eye. "Nothing to talk about just yet. I'm still ruminating on the details. I'll let you know when the time is right."

"Have you talked to Daddy about all of this?"

"Hmm? Oh not yet, but I'm sure he'll adjust to the news. He's lovely like that. Do hurry up, Katherine. We need to find you a new dress." She glanced up and down the street then lifted her arm, hailing a taxi.

"Dress for what?"

"Mr. Garcia's event tonight."

"Garcia's event? Mother, have you forgotten he's a gangster? We can't be seen in public with him!"

A taxi pulled up to the curb next to them.

Mrs. Karak rounded on her daughter with lightning reflexes. "You've already blundered down that avenue, haven't you? Well, now *we* have to make the best of *that* particular situation."

Katz gulped.

"The slightest shift in the wind can send the prey scampering. You have to be quick to pivot and chase down the best target that will benefit your cubs the most in the long run."

Mrs. Karak pulled the taxi door open and got in. Katz had little choice to follow or be left behind.

She'd messed up. Badly.

Dear Isis, how can I fix the mess this time?

Before her mother fixed things the way *she* wanted them?

———

At a quiet park with a lovely view of the ocean just outside of the city, an argument ensued...

"You're not leaving us behind," Bryah Lam snarled up at her boyfriend, Caleb Terry.

"I can't believe you spied on us, Bree," he growled back.

"You left us no choice, keeping us out of the loop."

"We're working an official FUC case. You're not agents yet," he said, exasperated.

She planted her fists on her hips, glaring up at him. "That hasn't stopped us from helping in crisis situations before. We're here, and we're helping."

Caleb straightened, glaring between the love of his life and his sister, Corra, who both glared right back.

"Dude, I'm with you on this, but we both know what they're like," Darcy said.

Caleb scowled at Zeek.

"Don't look at me, man. I had nothing to do with this."

Caleb scrubbed a hand over his face with a sigh, considering his options. "Of all the places to hide, Bree. Really? Under Zeek's truck seat? What if we had an accident?"

Bryah snorted. "Yeah? Well, it's just as well that my sense of smell sucks, because the noise coming out of you two after lunch was insane! I'm pretty sure I caught a buzz from all your fumes. I probably wouldn't have noticed an accident."

"Serves you right," Caleb said, red-faced.

"Okay, look, we have to figure out what's next," Darcy said, trying to keep his laughter in check. "Burritos?" he asked Bryah as an afterthought.

She nodded.

"I know your pain. At least it wasn't curry."

"Focus!" Caleb said.

"Bryah had one of Joe's micro-bugs. Works great, by the way. Very clear. Too clear," Corra said, then shot Bryah a glance, which made them both break out into giggles.

"So, you both eavesdropped on everything. Great." Caleb compressed his lips.

Uh-oh.

Bryah stopped giggling and got serious.

"Okay, well, if you're going into a fight arena and you need intel, let us help. We can keep watch. Just tell us who to keep our eyeballs on, and we've got you covered. Easy-peasy."

"No, *not* easy-peasy. Those guys aren't the kind of guys you want to notice you. And they will notice you—both of you."

"I'll be incognito. Squirrel-nito?" She shrugged. "And bugged. I'll go up high. They'll have those catwalk things for the scoreboard, right?"

Zeek rolled his eyes.

"What's your deal, King Kong Junior?"

"It's not a hockey arena, Bryah. It's an illegal fight ring."

"There might be some piping you can move across," Caleb said.

Zeek nodded. "Actually, I think someone mentioned Garcia was having a new lighting rig installed. Still. It won't be much cover."

Bryah shrugged. "Don't need much."

"Or much to hold on to. Nothing to hook your claws into if you slip. You might end up in the ring with the fighters."

"You could be trampled, especially in the shifted part of the fight. It gets pretty wild."

"Meh, I'm fast. Don't worry about me."

"Bree," Corra said, "maybe we should rethink this. This is

different than the last couple of times we, uhm, got into tight situations."

"Look, you guys, I get it. Be careful. Yadda yadda yadda, I know. I've been through all the safety training. My climbing and clinging have improved. And I've got the flying part pretty solid now since I've been taking lessons on how to use my new wings. I'm good. I'll be careful."

As a squirrel shifter with engineered wings, Bryah was determined to put these skills to good use as an agent-in-training. Sure, she wasn't a graduate—yet. She'd already proved herself capable when things got messy in the past, and she wasn't about to sit this one out too. Not when it concerned people she cared about.

This case meant a lot to Caleb. Since she'd met him, his main goal was to become a FUC agent so he could bring down the illegal fight rings he and Zeek had been forced into in their youth. There was no way she was going to be left behind on a case that was so important to him—not if she could help it.

"So, what's the plan?" Bryah asked.

"We just need to collect evidence proving Garcia is doing things illegally," Darcy said.

"With a focus on exploitation of shifters," Caleb added. "Otherwise, the human legal system could probably do the job —if they wanted to."

"More shifter profiteering by yet another shifter," Corra said, looking at Bryah.

"We know all too well that opportunists are going to opportune," Bryah added, rubbing Corra's shoulder. "Doesn't matter what kind of skin, fur, scales, or feathers they have."

Caleb turned his thoughtful gaze on Bryah and Corra. "Bryah, if you have any of Joe's micro-cameras, you can get images of everyone in attendance, while Darcy moves in on Garcia's social circle. Zeek and I will cover things from the fighters' side. Corra, you can blend in with the crowd where you can help Bryah's surveillance from a distance, but you both have to stay out of sight."

"Remember, Garcia is just as bad as your grandfather," Darcy warned Corra.

"And as the Old Man's main rival, he'll take advantage of any shot he can to rub our grandfather's nose in his failures. If he sees a chance to use you in any way, he will. So be careful," Zeek said to Corra.

"You too. All of you."

22

The small dressing room was dank, crowded, and stained.

The concrete walls did nothing to filter the loud music and shouts of the spectators surrounding the ring.

From the bench, Zeek glanced up at Caleb as he tightened the wraps on his wrists for him.

Neither spoke.

"Good?" Caleb nodded, jaw tight, toward the wrappings.

Zeek grunted.

Neither he nor Caleb had expected to be back in a place like this. Especially not voluntarily.

He knew Caleb wanted to be there even less than he did, but he also understood what it meant to him.

To himself, too.

Caleb had spent years trying to talk Zeek into quitting the ring—as he had done.

It had taken his grandfather threatening Corra's and Katz' well-being for him to decide.

This isn't going back.

He drew a deep breath, sucking in the stale, tangy scents of sweat and blood, fear and testosterone, letting it seep in.

He used to take a hit of some cheap drug before going out to add to the rush, dull the pain, and ramp up the adrenaline.

There's no going back.

"You know what you have to do?" Caleb asked.

Zeek nodded again. "I remember the rules. Man-fight three rounds. Shifter-fight till it's done."

"For years, Garcia's wanted you fighting for him. He won't be able to suppress his gloating." Caleb patted his shoulder, as though he were looking for something to say that wasn't an apology. "Your opponent's gonna be big. I just don't know which one you're up against."

"I know. Garcia is trying to prove his dominance. He's going to throw his biggest guy at us," he said, getting to his feet, bouncing and shaking out his limbs. "I just hope it's not a fucking rhino."

"I dunno, Zeek. That last one you fought you got a pretty good grip on his horn and gave him a good swing."

Zeek chuckled, leaning into a combination of stretches, and then he threw a few air punches and kicks.

The movements brought some of the muscle memory back. He welcomed the first trickles of adrenaline.

"Since we haven't got much of a choice in this, it'd be nice if we were in the ring together. Tag teaming like old times."

Caleb scooped up the rest of the tape and dropped it into his bag. "We fought well together."

We can do this.

His gorilla chuffed.

Now's the time to start the chest-beating again.

But his gorilla was disinterested.

Caleb glanced at his watch and snatched up a couple of water bottles and a med kit. "Time."

Zeek followed Caleb out of the dressing room and down the narrow, dingy hall toward the ring.

His gaze swept the audience, seeking, but hoping not to

find, Katz. Darcy had said she'd be in attendance with him, as per their mother's orders, which Zeek didn't understand and didn't like.

Where is she? Is she safe?

He shoved away negative thought after negative thought attacking his psyche.

I've gone soft.

I can't fight anymore.

I'm going to lose.

I'm going to lose, and I'm going to lose Caleb's chance to close his case.

His gorilla growled at his internal whining.

This would be easier if I could just take a hit of something before going out there.

Zeek's hands shook at his sides. He hadn't been in a ring fight without some sort of drug to bolster himself in years.

And Katz would be watching.

He was in better physical shape now than he'd ever been now that he was free of any drugs, but in this moment, at the edge of the ring crowd, he felt powerless. Useless.

Useless. Fuckup. Rollo's voice barked at him.

He flinched, turning.

Rollo was locked away in prison.

A tsunami of rage swept through Zeek, shuddering through him. His heart pounded as his fists clenched, and his vision blurred momentarily.

His gaze swept the audience again.

Would the violence frighten her? Disgust her?

Maybe that was best.

A layer of frustration rippled beneath the surface, overlaying the rage that still chugged through his veins, creating a potent combination.

Teeth grinding against the power of those two emotions, he

found her with Darcy, looking posh and bored, seated among others of their kind not far from Garcia.

His gaze landed on Garcia, who leaned toward one of his lackeys but looked at Katz.

The lackey approached Katz and Darcy to speak with them. They both rose and moved closer to Garcia.

His gorilla growled.

Caleb glanced at Zeek then followed his line of sight, sucking in a breath.

Success. Danger.

"Focus," Caleb said to Zeek, who'd begun to pace.

The crowd roared, punctuated by the pounding of the bell. The current fight was done. The loser was dragged away. The winner paraded around the ring and then was led away to be bandaged up.

Caleb leaned toward Zeek so he could be heard over the din. "They've made contact. It's just up to us to do our thing now. Keep Garcia's attention."

Show him we're still contenders.

Zeek represented the Terry family. This submission to fight made it look as though the Old Man was submitting to Garcia's superiority. With his mother as the matriarch of the family, it was up to him to do what was best for her.

Zeek was her right hand and would do anything to protect her from the machinations of this life.

If everything went well, he'd continue to help her bring the family into legitimate business.

Legitimacy didn't mean weakness.

And he was here to prove that as he stepped into the ring.

The ring announcer introduced him. The crowd cheered.

His opponent entered and took up his place across from Zeek and Caleb.

He was big. Bigger than Zeek.

His opponent assessed him with a lazy smirk, flexing.

Zeek sniffed.

"Fuck." His heart jack-hammered in his chest.

"Grizzly," Caleb said. "He's young, Zeek. Your experience will trump him."

"We're so fucked."

"No, we're not. I know you've got this, Zeek. You're the best fighter I've ever seen in these rings. When we fought together, we were unstoppable."

"That was a long time ago, man."

"Doesn't matter. We're Terrys. *You're* a Terry."

That statement twisted Zeek's heart as he glanced at Caleb's solemn expression.

He means it.

How long had Zeek felt like an outsider?

Hearing those words were like punches to his chest.

He stepped to the center of the ring, facing the younger, bigger grizzly shifter. The overhead lights brought everything into harsh reality.

The bell's shrill signal set the opponents to circle one another, taking test shots as they determined tactics.

The grizzly shifter started yammering.

Aw, Christ, he's a talker.

Maybe he'll wear himself out, wasting his energy talking.

Zeek could only hope.

The testing phase ended with an abrupt hard jab. Zeek took the hit to his jaw, backing away, giving ground as pain streaked up the side of his face. He shook it off, bringing his fists up higher.

He glanced toward Garcia's position on his dais. Katz was seated next to him now, Darcy on her other side. Her attention was turned on Garcia, while Darcy watched the fight with an air of boredom.

The distraction cost Zeek another hit to his ribs that momentarily took the air from his lungs.

"Focus!" Caleb yelled from the other side of the ropes.

From his periphery, Zeek saw Garcia's hand slide down Katz' thigh.

Zeek's gorilla snarled as he deflected a third hit and counter-punched the grizzly.

He kept the grizzly occupied for the full three rounds in human form. Circling. Giving ground, taking ground. He peered from a swollen eye. Blood flowed from his opponent's forehead and cheekbone.

They were both wearing down, and Zeek had to hope the tactic was enough to give him the chance he needed once they shifted.

23

Revulsion gurgled through Katz' gut as she deftly removed Garcia's clammy fingers from her naked thigh. She cleared her throat to cover the slip of her gag reflex.

Darcy reached for a glass of champagne from the tray set before them, handing it to her.

She offered him a look of thanks and forced herself not to guzzle the alcohol.

She needed to be clear-headed, but she also desperately needed a little booster to help her get through this event without breaking this guy's fingers and larynx.

Ugh, I need a bleach bath when this night is over. Darcy owes me for this ghoul gob. Big time.

She distracted herself with all the childish things she would make Darcy do to appease her.

Until Zeek stepped into view.

Bare-chested, hair tied at his nape, wrists wrapped in white tape, shorts dangerously low on his hips.

Her gaze slid all over his exposed flesh, letting the fantasies roll and forgetting about the mustachioed gob next to her that she was supposed to be distracting and enticing and getting to like her so that Darcy could get information out of him.

Wow, I suck at this, but oh, my Isis, Zeek looks munchable.

She downright wanted to nibble her way along every ridge and valley of muscle, especially the ones that disappeared below the waistband of his pants.

Mmm-mmm!

Katz readjusted her posture on her seat, which inadvertently leaned her closer to Garcia.

His gaze landed on her sky-lift bosom, then grinned up at her. "Later, sweetheart. I have stacks riding on this fight. You can roll in 'em with me after the fight."

Her stomach flipped, and all the squishy, yummy, sexy thoughts of Zeek popped as Garcia insinuated himself into her fantasies.

Gross.

She forced a smile and giggled and did everything in her power not to loosen her face. If she did, there'd be no hiding what she was really feeling.

It wasn't like this was the first time she'd had to play up to a jerk like this to gain information. But this guy was at the extreme end of how far she was willing to go.

Unfortunately, there was too much on the line here to wuss out.

It was just…seeing Zeek, like that, in all his manly yumminess, made the contrast painfully glaring.

Struggling for charming, she widened her smile. "Which one are you betting on?"

He snorted. "The bigger guy, of course."

Katz glanced back toward the ring as Zeek moved into his area and another shirtless guy moved in across from him.

Holy catnip! That guy was *way* bigger than Zeek. He was a mountain, and Zeek was no little hillock himself.

She swallowed hard, gaze flicking between the combatants.

"Oh my," she said.

Garcia patted her thigh again, a little higher each time. "You'll like this, sweetheart. Zeek LeBrute is good, but my guy is better. Bigger and younger. Trained him myself."

"Wow," she breathed, hoping she sounded awed enough.

The bell clanged, and the fight started.

She sat motionless, eyes locked on the ring. Locked on Zeek as he moved. She couldn't blink. Couldn't breathe.

After the first two hits, she didn't want to watch anymore, but she couldn't look away either.

Her heart hammered in her chest.

She truly was in awe, watching the brute force of the hits and the grace with which Zeek moved around the ring, drawing his opponent with him.

Garcia's hand remained firmly on her thigh.

On her other side, Darcy began drawing Garcia into stilted conversation, splitting his attention, inviting him to give away more information than he might normally have.

"I've heard Trent Aslan has been spending time here," Darcy said, engaging Garcia in idle gossip.

Katz listened in, curious to hear what they had to say on the matter.

Garcia snorted, eying Darcy. Then he chuckled with a shake of his head. "That guy is a wet sop. Poor loser."

"Poor loser?"

"Oof! Did you see that hit, sweetheart? That was a good one."

Katz' nails were firmly embedded in her palm, her chest locked so that air huffed in little gasps.

Zeek was backing his way around the ring. His opponent followed, throwing connecting punches.

She twitched with each hit.

The fighters went into a tangle where it looked as though they were hugging each other, sweating and panting.

The bell's shrill clang sent them to opposite corners.

Katz sucked in a breath.

"What was I saying? Oh yeah, young Aslan. Sore loser. He lost some money and trashed his place." Garcia made a disapproving clucking sound as he shook his head. "Poor show. I told him he should put his frustration to better use."

"Such as?" Darcy prompted with a casual sip of his drink, letting his gaze slide toward the ring as though only semi-interested in the gossip.

Garcia shrugged. "Working it out in the ring, like most men."

"Did he do it? Fight someone in the ring?" Katz asked, wide-eyed.

Garcia snorted. "Nah. Too much of a pussy. Lion, my ass," he added with a mutter.

"So where is he now?" Katz asked, blinking.

"Not far." He nodded toward a section at the far end of the place.

Katz followed his gaze and gulped.

Trent wasn't watching the fight. He was staring straight at her.

"Yeah, he made a request. I get 'em from time to time," he said cryptically.

She blinked at Garcia, encouraging him to elaborate. Leaning closer, she breathed, "What kind of request could he possibly ask of you?"

His eyes dropped to her generous cleavage. His fingers twitched on her thigh.

"To protect your honor, of course. I thought that was a little extreme, but I can see why he'd want to."

"Wha-what do you mean?"

"Vengeance. He wants to avenge the public insult LeBrute gave you. I heard all about it after I left the engagement party. I thought my presence would have been scandalous enough for your type, but it seems that kiss he planted on you rocked the social world."

Katz' thoughts bounced around her head, trying to make sense of what he was actually saying. Her gaze shot back to Zeek in the ring. His eye was swollen shut.

The fighters were pushed apart again with another sounding of the bell. How many rounds had that been? Two? Three? She wasn't sure.

"Avenge how?" Darcy's bored voice broke the hum growing in Katz' head as she struggled to control her spiking anxiety.

She looked to Garcia's face.

He leered at her.

"Aslan agreed to sell me a substantial chunk of his company's stock in repayment of the money he lost as well as this favor to his pride."

"What favor?" Katz asked, managing not to scream in frustration.

"Just a little, you know, near-manslaughter."

Her head whipped back toward the ring. "The fight?"

Garcia nodded and shrugged. "Things happen sometimes. Fight gets out of hand, and claws slip. Jaws snap a little too hard, that sort of thing."

Oh, Isis.

Nausea swarmed Katz' senses as the bell sounded again.

This time when the fighters returned to the center to battle, they weren't in man-form.

Zeek's gorilla burst out with a roar and beating of his chest.

His grizzly bear opponent met him roar for roar.

The two blasted each other in the face trying to intimidate the other.

"And you agreed to it?" Darcy asked, casual.

Katz noted the tightening of the muscles in his neck as he watched the scene below.

"Yeah, sure. The crowd loves that kind of drama. Only now

and then, mind you. Can't have them getting bored with the spectacle. Special occasions."

"And this is a special occasion?"

"Sure is." He grinned. "I'm working out a substantial deal with your mother. Now, that woman is one hell of a lioness." He winked. "Drives a hard bargain. Respect."

"You're working on a deal with our mother?" Darcy asked, allowing his curiosity to show.

"Well, since things seemed to have soured between your sister and the Aslan boy, your mother decided to barter for something better. Someone better. Solid. Wealthy. Powerful." He leaned closer to Katz.

"Oh" was all she could muster, quickly turning her face back toward the ring just as the grizzly took a swipe at Zeek. Fur flew through the air, and blood speckled the floor.

She gasped.

Zeek stumbled.

She hadn't noticed just how much bigger the grizzly was than Zeek's gorilla. Abnormally bigger. Claws longer. Too long for a normal beast.

"That guy doesn't look right," she said. "He looks…"

"Enhanced," Darcy said, voice clipped.

Just then, despite his wounds, Zeek sidestepped another swipe of ridiculously long claws and ducked behind the over-sized grizzly with a roll and a spin. He came up with his hands wrapped around the grizzly's ankle with enough force to flip him on his face.

Big claws? Yes.

Opposable thumbs? No.

Zeek gripped hard and began to drag him with all his strength, turning with a grunt, tossing him against the far corner.

The grizzly hit the corner hard and at an awkward angle, which would have disabled a lesser beast.

Instead, he bounced and came back at Zeek, meaning to shred him.

Midway across the ring, something dropped from the spotlights suspended above.

The grizzly roared, reaching for his face as that *something* spun like a furry fury and let out a tiny scream.

"Shit!" Darcy shot to his feet.

"What's happening?" Katz screamed, terrified.

Everything happened so fast. Katz blinked, and next she knew, Caleb had shifted into his dog and launched himself into the ring.

The grizzly's claws connected with the back of Zeek's shoulder.

"Just getting rid of the competition," Garcia said with a smirk as he looked at Katz with sly eyes, which suddenly widened when she began growling.

No thoughts registered.

She became pure instinct.

Her clothes disappeared, replaced by silky sandy fur as she launched forward.

She was no lioness, but her teeth were sharp. And accurate.

Garcia's oily throat convulsed between her jaws.

The scent of his fear spiked so that she tasted it, sour against her tongue.

She could feel his indecision. Shift and risk a jugular puncture in order to put her in her place. Or stay still until his men could subdue her.

She continued to growl.

Garcia's men jumped into position around them, aiming their weapons at Katz and Darcy, ignoring the chaos that suddenly broke out around the ring as swarms of agents moved in.

The grizzly continued to swipe at Zeek, who still struggled against the unnatural beast, holding him at bay with Caleb's help. By now, Corra's dog form was in view, next to her brother, guarding the tiny squirrel shifter and helping to defend Zeek.

The points of Katz' teeth punctured Garcia's flesh, and she tasted blood.

He went even more rigid.

"You should call off your grizzly and your men," Darcy advised. "My sister is deadly when she's pissed."

Garcia's hand moved a fraction, and his men backed off. He moved again, and someone gave a shrill whistle. The grizzly's growling and snarling ceased.

Darcy's warm fingers gently stroked her scruff.

She eased her jaws, releasing Garcia, giving her head a shake to get the gross taste of him off her tongue.

Damn. Her new dress was a shredded mess on the floor. *I really liked that one.*

Seeing her attention on the fabric, Darcy said, "I'll get you a new one. I owe you."

You bet you do. Big time.

She snorted, turned away, and leaped her way to the ring, which was surrounded by a crowd.

Shouldering knees aside, she squeezed her way toward Zeek, still in his gorilla form, slouched against the side of the ring, panting.

She scented his blood and pain.

He remained shifted to speed the healing.

"Dr. Nolan is on his way," Miranda Brownsmith said from somewhere behind Katz.

Katz approached Zeek, licked his face, and curled up in his lap.

His large hand found the fur on her head and shoulders.

She began to purr, and he relaxed against her with a sigh.

She looked up to see Garcia and Trent and his friends being led away by Caleb, dressed in FUC-issue sweats with Bryah in her squirrel form seated on his shoulder, chittering at the grizzly, paw raised.

Was that a middle digit?

Darcy had followed Katz to check on Zeek's condition. He grinned at them. "Joe's going to go over the recordings right away. Garcia's boasts about accepting money from Aslan to take Zeek out will be his downfall."

Her purr rumbled louder. They'd done it. And she had helped Darcy with his first big case.

As for what was going to happen with Zeek? She had no idea.

She no longer knew what her mother had planned for her. She didn't care.

The teaching job at the Academy was supposed to be temporary—an experiment to prove to herself she could be independent. Maybe her independence should be permanent.

Glancing up at Zeek's gorilla face, she nestled closer.

Independence would wait till tomorrow.

She had a gorilla to take care of today.

24

A WEEK LATER...

Katz pulled the door to The Hub open and strode inside.

Tonight, they were celebrating Caleb and Darcy's success in bringing Garcia in.

She bypassed Bear, the pub's proprietor, with a wave and found her brother in the back room with everyone else, drinks in hand.

Darcy's face lit up at her arrival. He leaned in to kiss her cheek. "Thanks for coming."

Caleb turned toward her with a grin and held up his drink. "To Katz."

She laughed as everyone saluted her with their drink and cheered.

"Glad to help out."

Corra bumped her shoulder. "Where've you been all week? We missed you in class."

Katz shrugged. "Had to take some time off and do some negotiating."

"Your mother?" Corra lifted a brow.

"Yep."

"How'd that go?" Bryah asked, moving closer and slipping her arm around Caleb's waist. He pulled her against him.

"Well..." Katz hesitated and turned her gaze to Darcy. "Mummy and Daddy aren't going to arrange a marriage for me either."

"Holy shit—you're kidding!" Darcy gaped.

"I know how much work Daddy put into researching and Mummy into the negotiations. And at the time, the match probably would have been a good one. But"—she shrugged— "Trent made choices that led him down a different path. And I've changed. People change. Plans should, too."

In fact, she'd gone into serious negotiations with her parents—specifically her mother.

Katz informed her that she would choose her own mate. She also warned that if there was interference in Darcy and Corra's relationship in order to influence Katz, that they would risk losing Darcy for good and Katz too.

Her mother's vision of a united family would crumble under her tight-fisted control.

A year ago, Katz would have never dreamed of opposing her parents' wishes. She'd been fully on board with their plans.

Now...

A gust of fresh spring air circulated through the pub, drawing her attention to the front door.

She turned to see Zeek talking to Bear before his eyes found hers.

Last she saw him he had been settled comfortably in the Academy infirmary under the care of Dr. Manners. She hadn't left his side until then.

Darcy and Corra had texted her updates on Zeek's condition and progress while she was away.

"Hey, stranger," he said, eyes on hers. "Back to finish out the class?"

"Of course."

Caleb asked, "How was your meeting with the Old Man?"

"Intense."

"Isn't it always?"

Zeek blew out a breath and nodded.

"And?" Corra prompted.

"What did he say?" Caleb pushed.

"He signed the papers." Zeek grinned.

"Holy shit!" Caleb's face lit with excitement.

"That's awesome!" Corra hugged her cousin.

"What papers?" Katz asked, looking from Zeek to Caleb and Corra.

"The Old Man signed over control of all of his assets to my mother after I told him that Caleb successfully closed his case. Mom is sorting through the paperwork. There were all kinds of investments that no one knew about. She is one wealthy lady now."

"That's fantastic, Zeek! Now she can work on that charity she was talking about."

"And you don't need to do double time between the training and the Academy to help her bring in income," Corra said.

"Don't *have* to but will continue anyway. The Academy is growing on me. I blame you for the do-good bug, Caleb."

"Feels great, doesn't it?" Caleb grinned.

"Yeah. Yeah it does."

"Have there been updates on the fighters that were taken in along with Garcia?" Bryah asked, sipping her beer.

"Yeah, actually. Now that Garcia's been taken in, some of them rolled on him. Not all, as we'd expected. The grizzly Zeek was fighting was indeed an experiment survivor that somehow got Garcia's notice. Apparently, Garcia had blackmailed him into fighting for him with threats of turning him over to FUC. He had the poor guy convinced that FUC would terminate him, whereas Garcia said he would do all he could to protect him—so long as he earned his keep."

Bryah growled.

Caleb squeezed her close.

Katz smiled, taking in the affection between the two. Darcy and Corra also stood close, hands clasped as they talked with them. The rest of the Hub was full of revelers. Some of her students were enjoying the pool table and dartboard in the back.

"Is that Knife-flipper with Lydia?" She nodded toward the pair, who seemed to be in an intimate conversation at a nearby booth.

"Sure is," Bryah said. "Vo and Lydia make a cute couple. Looks like everyone is finding their special person." She winked at Katz and grinned at Zeek.

Katz' heart flip-flopped. She looked up at Zeek.

Zeek glanced at his watch. "Congratulations again, guys. I just wanted to tell you the news about the Old Man. I have next week's curriculum to plan."

"We couldn't have done it without the two of you helping," Caleb said, giving Zeek a big hug.

Zeek's throat worked as he thumped his cousin's back, returning the hug.

Katz knew how much this moment meant to him. Katz had never seen Caleb be anything but grumpy and reserved with Zeek. She blinked away tears at seeing the cousins reconciled.

Caleb released Zeek and kissed Katz' cheek. "Thank you."

She grinned. "Oh, you're very welcome. Darcy owes me big, starting with a new dress or two. And a spa day to counteract the dry skin I have after multiple bleach baths to get that slimy guy's funk off my skin."

"Can I get you a French 75?" Bryah asked Katz.

"No, I'm heading out, too. I have a lot of catching up to do before classes resume on Monday."

"I'll walk you out," Zeek offered.

She nodded, and they said their goodbyes to everyone and waved to Bear on their way out to the parking lot.

He held the door for her to exit first.

The outside air swirled his scent around her. She drew in a deep breath. Gorilla, leather, Zeek.

Zeek held the door for Katz, breathing in the scent of her. Feline, peony, Katz.

His heart pounded in his chest as she stepped past him. She descended the steps, striding to the end of the building. She turned to look back at him.

He released the door to join her. The nearby streetlight illuminated her features.

His chest tightened, hampering his breathing.

Is this it?

Aslan was no longer an issue, but that didn't mean her mother wouldn't force her into a new contract. Katz wouldn't jeopardize Darcy and Corra's shot at happiness.

He glanced at the hotel behind her.

So many memories there.

They still had some time together until their contracts at the Academy were up for renewal.

"Hey, anything to do in this hick town?" she said.

He blinked, turning his attention back to her face. Her gold-green eyes glittered in the low light.

The left corner of her lips tilted up.

"Me."

Her gaze dropped to his feet and slid up his body.

He hardened under her inspection.

She grinned, stepping forward. "Let's see if Carl still has my card on file."

Zeek's hands drifted up Katz' arms to cradle her face. He drank in every inch of her lovely features. "One more night?"

She shook her head. "I was hoping for something a little more... long term?"

The question made his heart ache then pound with the realization of what she was saying.

"Long term? What about your parents?"

"We had a little chat. Got Dad on my side, and we made Mother see reason."

"You're kidding."

"Not only am I free to choose who I want to be with, but I also have a seat on the board, too."

"So she's finally recognizing how amazing you are."

Katz laughed. "She said she was waiting for me to step up and see it myself."

Zeek snorted. "I'll never understand that woman."

"My father is the only one that does. That's why they're so perfect together."

Zeek's fingers stroked her cheekbones. "As are we."

"We are," she whispered. The tip of her tongue slid over her lip invitingly.

He leaned down, touching his mouth to hers with all the gentleness in his heart.

She had no idea just how incredible she was to him.

His kitten.

His little hiss.

She broke the kiss with a gasp. "Zeek. Let's go."

She grabbed his hand, tugging him toward the old hotel, running in her three-inch heels as though she were barefoot.

He had no choice but to follow.

And follow her he would, so long as she wanted him.

Anywhere. Always.

The End.

NOT QUITE! There are more FUC Academy books coming!

To find out more about these books and more, visit worlds.EveLanglais.com or sign up for the EveL Worlds newsletter. If you haven't already downloaded the **free Academy intro** (written by Eve Langlais) make sure you grab it at worlds.evelanglais.com/wordpress/book/fucacademy1!

ALSO BY JODI KENDRICK

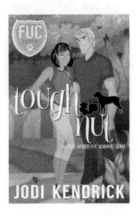

TOUGH NUT

Bryah Lam, living on the fringes of the shifter community is determined to unite her best friend with her long lost family, even if that means blowing through all her savings and going to the far side of the country to do it.

Caleb Terry finally has the chance to create a life of purpose and stability for himself through his enrolment at the Furry United Coalition Newbie Academy, and he's determined to keep it that way. Simple and uncomplicated.

Until Bryah shows up disrupting Caleb's budding 'simple life'.

Buy Now

DIAMOND IN THE RUFF

Corra Terry is a newly enrolled cadet at the Furry United Coalition Academy alongside her BFF Bryah Lam. After her experiences at the hands of Bryah's crazy ex-boyfriend, Corra has decided that becoming a FUC agent is the best way to get dangerous shifters like him off the streets. And nosy, arrogant tomcats have no place in her plans.

Ladies' man, Darcy Karak is enjoying the single life while training to become an agent. When his roommate's sister enrolls at the Academy, his curiosity gets the better of him and he can't help his sudden determination to teach Corra how to have some fun - if he can ignore her bark and evade her bite.

Buy Now

HONEYED NUT

A kid, a second chance, and a mystery chicken.

Minutes after Bear learns he's a daddy, he's sent on a mission to Hong Kong… the very city where his ex resides. He insists that bears don't fly, but there's no getting out of it. An addled groundhog needs help, and he's the only one for the job.

Maggie Lam returns home after a long day at work to find a second chance seated in her living room. The years haven't curbed the passion that sizzled between Bear and Maggie and they're still drawn together, despite the complications that had forced them apart in the first place.

But before they can figure out if they have a future with each other, they have to connect the dots between missing shifters in Maggie's neighborhood, and a mysterious chicken the groundhog claims to have followed there.

Buy Now

ABOUT THE AUTHOR

Jodi Kendrick is an author living in Eastern Ontario with her family. A history enthusiast and word dabbler most of her life, she enjoys exploring 'beyond-the-everyday' and the 'time-before-now', discovering relationship threads weaving individuals through time and place. She writes fantasy romance, historical romance and sometimes delves into horror, dark fantasy, speculative and paranormal. She's rarely seen without flashy notebooks and colourful pens.

Follow Jodi Kendrick at:

Website: jodikendrick.com
Newsletter Sign-Up: jodikendrick.com
Twitter: @JKendrickAuthor
Instagram: instagram.com/jkendrickauthor
Facebook: facebook.com/JodiKendrickAuthor
Good Reads: goodreads.com/jodikendrick
BookBub: bookbub.com/authors/jodi-kendrick